Michael Underwood and The Murder Room

››› This title is part of The Murder Room, our series dedicated to making available out-of-print or hard-to-find titles by classic crime writers.

Crime fiction has always held up a mirror to society. The Victorians were fascinated by sensational murder and the emerging science of detection; now we are obsessed with the forensic detail of violent death. And no other genre has so captivated and enthralled readers.

Vast troves of classic crime writing have for a long time been unavailable to all but the most dedicated frequenters of second-hand bookshops. The advent of digital publishing means that we are now able to bring you the backlists of a huge range of titles by classic and contemporary crime writers, some of which have been out of print for decades.

From the genteel amateur private eyes of the Golden Age and the femmes fatales of pulp fiction, to the morally ambiguous hard-boiled detectives of mid twentieth-century America and their descendants who walk our twenty-first century streets, The Murder Room has it all. **›››**

The Murder Room
Where Criminal Minds Meet

themurderroom.com

Michael Underwood (1916–1992)

Michael Underwood (the pseudonym of John Michael Evelyn) was born in Worthing, Sussex and educated at Christ Church College, Oxford. He was called to the Bar in 1939 and served in the British army during World War Two. He returned to work in the Department of Public Prosecutions until his retirement in 1976, and wrote almost 50 crime novels informed by his career in the law. His five series characters include Sergeant Nick Atwell and lawyer Rosa Epton, of whom is was said by the *Washington Post* that she 'outdoes Perry Mason'.

Adam's Case

Michael Underwood

An Orion book

Copyright © Isobel Mackenzie 1961

The right of Michael Underwood to be identified as the author of this
work has been asserted in accordance with the Copyright, Designs and
Patents Act 1988.

This edition published by
The Orion Publishing Group Ltd
Orion House
5 Upper St Martin's Lane
London WC2H 9EA

An Hachette UK company
A CIP catalogue record for this book is available from the British Library

ISBN 978 1 4719 0780 7

www.orionbooks.co.uk

To John and Janet McCormick

CHAPTER ONE

'Y OU DON'T look a bit like a barrister. I just can't picture
you in a wig.'
    Elsie Dunn's tone was more puzzled than dis-
appointed. The scene of her reproach was the refreshment
room of St. Pancras Station on a warm, wet Sunday evening
in June : its object Adam Cape, aged twenty-five, single and
barrister-at-law.

As the girl spoke, she fixed Adam with a nervous eager
gaze which caused him to look quickly elsewhere, first at the
brown pools of spilt tea on the table between them and then
at his shoes whose lack of shine seemed in keeping with his
present mood.

'Shall I be seeing you again ?' she asked anxiously.

'I hope not', Adam would have replied if this hadn't
sounded unkind. The week-end had not been a success and
now he was waiting only to see her train steam out before
writing finis to the whole short-lived episode.

'Who knows !' he said unsatisfactorily, with the sad,
dreamy smile behind which he took refuge at such moments;
moments, that is, of being pressed by girl-friends for a
declaration of devotion.

No, the week-end had been a bore, and the irony of it was
that it had been Sara's pressing invitation to go and spend it
with her people in Norfolk which had made him invent a

1

distant cousin just arrived from the West Indies whom he must stay in town and be nice to.

He liked Sara a lot and enjoyed going out with her, but recently she had begun to display proprietorial airs which he had felt must be resisted.

He looked at his watch. 'We'd better go, Elsie' – he winced as he spoke her name – 'trains are apt to get packed on Sunday evenings and you don't want to have to stand all the way, do you?'

Aware that the girl was watching him closely, almost as if she was determined to memorize every pore of his skin, he got up, seized her bag and led the way out.

He had hoped that she would suggest his leaving once she'd found a seat on the train, but it was soon apparent that nothing was further from her mind.

For twenty minutes they stood making pointless conversation until finally the guard blew his whistle.

'I have enjoyed myself, Adam', she said feverishly as she leant towards him through the carriage window.

'I'm so glad. So have I.' He could afford to be magnanimous now that the train was actually moving.

'You weren't offended at my saying that about your not looking like a barrister?'

'Of course not.' He fixed a smile on his face. ''Bye. Have a good journey.'

Adam waved while he counted up to three, then turned and walked rapidly down the platform. Elsie Dunn was at last safely on her way back to Leicester, and it certainly wouldn't be his invitation which would bring her to London again. But that's what came of inviting out girls on the strength of a pair of shapely legs but a less than short acquaintance.

Almost the only perceptive thing she had said the whole week-end had been her remark about his not looking like a barrister. For not only did he not bear any resemblance to Elsie's imagined picture of one, but he didn't even look like the genuine standard article to be seen and heard around the courts.

Indeed, Adam frequently wondered how he had come to embrace the Bar as a profession, since he felt that he lacked most of the requisite qualities for success. But whenever he pointed this out across five thousand miles of water to his parents in Barbados, he was invariably reminded how his uncle, who had been a famous Q.C. but was now dead, had said precisely the same thing to his parents thirty years before.

'Do stick at it a bit longer, darling', his mother had written in her last letter. 'It's such a fine profession and we're so keen you should succeed and quite certain that you will if only you keep going. I can so well remember your Uncle Godfrey being in despair at ever getting started and look where he finished up' – in a premature grave, Adam had reflected sardonically – 'I'm sure the briefs will come tumbling in once people have had a chance to see you in court. I enclose a cheque for £50 as a small *douceur*. . . .'

Adam had read the letter, sighed and gone out to cash the cheque.

The clock in the main hall of St. Pancras showed twenty minutes past six as he passed through on his way out of the station. The very hour, he reflected, that Sara's train would be arriving at Liverpool Street, which meant that in about

3

half an hour's time she would almost certainly be ringing him.

He decided, nevertheless, that before returning to his room in Kensington he must go for a swim. For Adam, swimming was an elixir. It refreshed his body and revived his spirit. Having been brought up in the West Indies, he had learnt to swim as soon as he could walk.

' 'Ello, Mr. Cape', the grizzled attendant at the baths greeted him, showing the respect due to his most regular and proficient customer. 'Not wet enough for you outside, isn't it – going to 'ave a swim?' He handed Adam a key to a locker, and a few minutes later was watching with silent pleasure the short powerful legs and slim arms driving the lithe body through the smooth satin water.

Adam did four lengths without a pause, then clambered out and shaking himself like a dog accepted the towel which the attendant handed him.

'I had a body like yours once, Mr. Cape', he said in a half wistful tone as Adam ran a hand through his tousled hair.

Adam laughed. 'Five feet six of skin and bone.'

'Wish I had muscles like yours now', the attendant went on, gazing at Adam's midriff. 'Ever do any boxing?'

'A bit at school. I must go and get dressed, George. Get us another dry towel.'

Ten minutes later with the feeling of elation a swim always brought him, Adam emerged into the rain and caught a bus back to Kensington.

'Your young lady's been ringing you, Mr. Cape', said Miss Brown, his landlady, as he was about to climb the stairs to his room. 'I told her I didn't know when you'd be back and she said would you call her when you get in.'

'Thanks, Miss B.'

'You're welcome, Mr. Cape.'

Since Miss Brown's phone was situated where her tenants could listen to one another's calls with the minimum of inconvenience, Adam usually chose to go to a public callbox round the corner from where he lived.

Without going up to his room, he now turned about and left the house. Sara, who shared a flat in Chelsea with two other girls, answered immediately.

'Hello, Sara, it's Adam. Miss B. says you've been ringing.' As he spoke he wriggled himself into a comfortable position inside the call-box in preparation for a lengthy siege.

'I looked out for you at Liverpool Street but I suppose you couldn't make it', Sara said. 'How was your cousin?'

'Dim. But she's gone now.'

'Gone! I thought she'd come over for several months.'

'I mean she's left London. She's training to be a nurse or something at Leicester.'

'Why Leicester?'

'What's wrong with Leicester?'

'It seems a funny place to come all the way from the West Indies to go to.'

'Well, that's where she's gone', Adam replied firmly.

'Did you have a very dull week-end with her?'

'Very.'

'Poor sweet! But I think it was terribly noble of you to stay in town and look after her.'

'Oh well, you know how it is with family . . .' Adam said uncomfortably and decided it was time to steer the conversation into less perilous channels before Sara's questions became more awkward or her sympathy too embarrassing.

He gave a little shiver as he suddenly pictured her finding out that the cousin from the West Indies was none other than Elsie Dunn of Leicester whom he had invited to town for the week-end on the strength of having met her casually in a bar a few weeks before. The fact that Elsie had been a bore, that not even her legs had been as good as he remembered them, and that the week-end had been a dreary failure from beginning to end could scarcely be claimed in his favour.

A quarter of an hour later, however, when he rang off, Adam had again reached the point of thinking that it would be rather nice if he were to be married to Sara. As he walked back to his room, he pondered the prospect further, and continued doing so as he lay on his bed smoking a cigarette.

Well, maybe one day he would ask her to marry him. Meanwhile, however, he supposed that he had to make his way in the law.

At the thought of chambers the next day, his heart sank a little. The brotherhood of the law, like the public school system, required that you should be a conformer in order to make life tolerable. But though Adam was sure he was a normal, friendly young man, he knew that he was not a conformer.

With a sigh, he rolled off the bed, undressed and a few minutes later was fast asleep.

CHAPTER TWO

SHORTLY after ten o'clock the next morning, Adam arrived at chambers prepared for another day of enervating idleness. Poking his head round a door, he greeted William, the chambers' clerk with a cheerful grin.

'Good morning, William.' The clerk looked up, seemed to be distracted by something about Adam's appearance and sorrowfully shook his head. 'What's wrong with me now?'

'Your hair, Mr. Cape . . .'

'That all? I'll comb it.'

'If only you'd wear a hat like all the other gentlemen.'

Adam raised an admonitory hand. 'Enough, William. I've given way to you on everything else, but I will not wear a hat, at least not the sort you want me to wear. If you want to know what I'd look like in a bowler, picture a monkey in one and take it from me that I'd look even sillier than that.' He brandished a neatly rolled umbrella. 'This is my badge of professional respectability. At least it doesn't make me feel the little snot one of your black hats would.' He gave the umbrella a casual twirl. 'Anything else before I go and get on with the crossword?'

In a drier than usual tone, the clerk said, 'There's a brief on your table awaiting your attention, Mr. Cape.'

'A brief!'

'It arrived on Friday afternoon after you'd left. You went early, you remember?'

The event was rare enough for Adam to feel momentarily stunned. To think that while he'd sloped off to meet Elsie, someone had actually delivered him a brief.

'What is it? A poor person's divorce? A legal aid at sessions?'

'Neither', William replied primly. 'It's a Yard brief to prosecute at the Bailey.'

Adam stared at his clerk in stupefaction. 'Gosh, I have gone up in the world.'

William smiled thinly. 'You'd better go and read it, sir. They may want to have a conference.'

'When's it for?'

'The case'll come on in the session starting a week tomorrow.'

This was the first time that anybody had hired Adam's forensic services for anything so important. His few previous appearances in the criminal courts had been prosecuting in minor motoring cases, or defending in the sort of case which was a lost cause from the beginning and in which either nothing could go wrong or nobody cared very much if it did. The sort of case in which the only room for speculation was whether the prisoner would get three or five years and in which he'd have been quite thankful to have got away with seven.

But this was something quite different, a definite move up the professional ladder. Or so he felt as he flung open the door of the tiny room which he shared with Charles Imrey.

Imrey was six years his senior and possessed almost everything that Adam lacked, including an elegant bowler hat which he wore tilted slightly forward over his forehead. Moreover, he had the beginnings of a steady practice and was always dashing from one court to another and giving the impression of working at high pressure.

When Adam entered the room, Imrey was bent over a set of papers, and others – Adam sometimes wondered if they weren't dummy sets – lay scattered about his desk.

'Hello, Charles, have a pleasant week-end?'

From the grunted reply, Adam knew that Imrey had noticed the brief on his table and was not pleased. Only the week before he had let slip that he considered he should be on the Yard list for police prosecutions.

Adam sat down and gazed happily at the slim bundle of papers which lay before him in isolated prominence. The outside of the brief informed him that he was to appear on behalf of the Commissioner of Police for the Metropolis in the prosecution of one Frankie Young.

Mesmerized by the prospect that the case might last two or three days and lead to that additional remuneration known delightfully as refreshers, Adam slipped off the piece of white tape to open the brief and discover who Frankie Young was and what he was supposed to have done.

'At the time of the offence,' Adam read, 'Young was employed as a storeman by Mather Brothers Ltd., printers, of Packhorse Road, N.10. . . .'

His eye sped on down the page to learn what the offence was. Stated bleakly, it was wounding with intent, contrary to Section 18 of the Offences Against the Person Act 1861, the object of the attack being said to be Carole Young.

'Do I gather you've got a brief there, Adam?' Imrey asked languidly, looking in Adam's direction.

'A prosecution at the Bailey next week.'

'Not the case of Young by any chance?'

'Yes.'

'Oh well, we should have a good scrap, I'm defending.' Adam's jaw dropped and Charles Imrey laughed. 'Don't look so surprised. Young's solicitors phoned on Friday afternoon to inquire if I'd be available to take the case. They're a firm I've done quite a bit of work for', he added airily. 'Though between you and me, they're a bit fly and William's not too keen on them. However, he told them I'd only do the case for a corking fee and since they agreed to his figure without demur, it's Imrey for the Defence.'

Though Adam had grown used to Charles Imrey lording it over him he found this latest turn of events distinctly disagreeable. Indeed, he would sooner have heard that the Attorney General was defending, if that had been possible. The prospect of Imrey with his greater experience and commanding self-assurance needling him throughout the trial, as he most certainly would take every opportunity of doing, made Adam feel quite weak inside.

He could just hear him, after his client had been acquitted, saying in his most condescending tones, 'Expected you to put up a better scrap, Adam. You made a mistake, you know, in not re-examining the wife and your final speech to the jury lacked punch. Anyway, let's hope it won't prevent the Yard sending you further work.'

One of the cherished notions of the Bar is that two barristers can spend all day exchanging body blows in the forensic arena and at the end leave court together in an aura of professional comradeship.

Maybe it could happen, but Adam was more than certain

that it wasn't even an outside prospect in the case of the Queen against Young – whatever the result.

Bending over his brief again with renewed purpose he made a silent vow to get Mister Young convicted at all costs. Not only should justice be done, but Charles Imrey should be undone. A quick read of his papers convinced Adam that the two were compatible.

Any ideas he might have had about the case lasting several days were soon dispelled when he saw that there were only four witnesses for the prosecution.

The first was Carole Young who turned out to be the wife of the accused man. Next was a doctor with the euphonious name of Bill Jumbo who testified about the shoulder wound from which he found Mrs. Young to be suffering and which had apparently required the insertion of stitches. Then there was a police constable who'd been called to the Youngs' flat after the offence and lastly Detective-Sergeant Perry who had investigated the case and whose evidence consisted mostly of his interview with the accused.

It was this that Adam read first, scanning it for some indication that Frankie Young had already thrown in the sponge and was merely waiting for the prison gates to close behind him.

His eye alighted on the last line of the Detective-Sergeant's deposition. 'I cautioned and charged him with the offence and he replied, "Not guilty. I've told you it was an accident." '

Adam sighed and wrinkled his nose which had begun to tickle. Then lighting a cigarette he turned to the document labelled 'Exhibit 5' which was the accused's written state-ment under caution. The document which in nine cases out

11

of ten becomes a sort of Bridge of Sighs for its hapless author, paving his irrevocable path to prison.

But one look at this statement showed Adam that Young had said nothing he would later regret or would need to retract. It was a short statement and read as follows :

'We had been having a bit of a quarrel about money matters when my wife suddenly picked up the knife from the table. I told her not to be silly and to put it down but she started waving it about. I went to take it from her and in the struggle she got stabbed. It was a complete accident and the knife was never in my hand at any time. I went to phone a doctor and when I came back, I found a policeman there and my wife saying I'd stabbed her on purpose which is a lie. It happened just as I've said it did. This statement has been read over to me and is true.' There followed his signature.

If this *was* true, it followed that Carole Young's evidence could not be, and Adam turned again to her deposition.

It read : 'A quarrel began and suddenly my husband seized a knife, the one I use for vegetables, and came for me. I tried to get out of the way and the next thing I felt was a sudden pain in my shoulder and I saw the blood. My husband dashed out and a little later I went to the street door. I saw a policeman along the street and spoke to him. My husband didn't say anything before he attacked me. My shoulder is now all right apart from still being sore and stiff.'

Adam pursed his lips. This was the evidence on which the charge rested and it had an ominously indefinite ring about it. Admittedly Carole Young said her husband picked up the knife and came for her, but that was followed by a film-like dissolve in her evidence . . . 'The next thing I

12

felt . . .' He could just hear Charles Imrey's languid and arrogant tones boring away to enlarge this bolthole for his client. 'Thought you'd have put up a better scrap, Adam.'

Adam turned to his 'instructions', the particular points which the Solicitor to the Metropolitan Police, who had prepared the brief, thought Counsel should have in mind.

'Counsel will see,' the instructions ran, 'that the case rests entirely on the evidence of the wife who is, as Counsel will know' – as a matter of fact Adam didn't – 'not only a competent but a compellable witness for the prosecution. Though there is no reason to doubt the truth of her evidence, she does not give the impression of being a very strong witness and will require careful handling in the witness-box . . . Finger-print examination of the knife has been made with negative result . . . Counsel will observe from the antecedents report that the accused has previous convictions for dishonesty. . . .'

'Hello, Adam, hear you've got a prosecution at the Bailey next session.' The speaker who had just stuck his head round the door was Robert Canfield, who was one of the more senior members of chambers.

'Yes, quite a tricky one too. Hope I don't make a mess of it.'

Canfield shook his head in a gesture of mild deprecation.

'I don't think anyone worries very much what happens in these domestic biff-baffs, provided nobody's actually killed or permanently disabled. Anyway, mind you give Charles a good run for his money.' He seemed about to add something further, but then with a casual flip of the hand was gone.

From the passage outside, Imrey's voice floated in. 'Been hearing about Adam's case?'

A determined expression came into Adam's eyes as he sat back in his chair. Adam's case! Imrey had spoken with amused condescension as though to rank the event as one of the year's more diverting. Well, he'd show him.

By the time he went out to lunch, he had read his brief through four times and knew large portions of it by heart. Before eating he phoned the travel bureau where Sara worked and asked for her extension.

'Fastwork Travel, good afternoon, may I help you?'

'It's Adam.'

Her voice dropped to a conspiratorial whisper. 'Hello, darling.'

'O.K. to talk?'

'Yes, I've just finished with a client.'

'I'm doing a case at the Old Bailey next week, a prosecution. I thought you'd like to know.'

Sara was indeed delighted to know and showered congratulations on him. She even spoke of taking the day off to come and hear him, but this was pushing enthusiasm too far and Adam received the suggestion coolly.

After lunch in Hall, where he sat next to a barrister who immediately button-holed him and talked interminably about a recent decision of the Court of Appeal in a case of which Adam had never heard, he returned to chambers and read his brief a couple more times.

It was around four o'clock that his clerk brought him a letter, which had arrived by the afternoon post. It was addressed in a childish hand to 'Mr. Adam Cape, 3 Gray's Buildings, Temple, E.C.4.'

Inside was a single sheet of paper which bore writing in the same hand and which read as follows:

14

'Dear Sir,

'Carole Young is lying and you shouldn't believe her story. I know. I thought I ought to tell you this so as you won't press the case on perjured evidence. Sorry that I must remain anonymous, but please don't ignore this letter.'

At first Adam thought it must be a practical joke, though he couldn't think of anyone he knew who lived in the North London district of the postmark. Finally, it was the unfunniness of the letter and its faint air of threat that persuaded him to treat it seriously.

Luckily Charles Imrey was out, so he could use the phone without embarrassment. After speaking to someone in the Solicitor's branch at Scotland Yard he was put through to the division in which Detective-Sergeant Perry was stationed.

'Hello, sir, I thought you might call me', Sergeant Perry said cheerfully, after Adam had been connected with one extension after another. 'It's about the Young case, isn't it?'

'Yes, I've just received an anonymous letter about it. I thought I'd better let you know.'

'Too right, sir, too right', Sergeant Perry rejoined heartily. 'We get them all the time of course, but it's a bit off to start pestering counsel. What's it all about, sir?'

'I'd better read it to you', Adam said without enthusiasm. He found Detective-Sergeant Perry a shade too breezy. 'Here it is . . .'

'Hold on a tick, sir! What's the postmark on the envelope?' Adam told him. 'That's in this divisional area. O.K. go ahead, sir.'

Adam read the letter through without further interruption and was gratified by the silence which fell at the other end of the line.

'Well, sir', Sergeant Perry said at last. 'I don't quite know what to make of that.'

'It would appear to have been sent by someone rooting for the accused, but is there anything in the suggestion that she is lying, do you think?'

'No, sir, I'm sure she's told the truth about what happened.' He paused. 'Though I think rather more took place than what she has told us.'

'What do you want me to do about the letter?'

'I'd better have it, sir. I'll make a few inquiries, though I don't suppose I'll get anywhere. I'll send someone to collect it from your chambers tomorrow.'

'Perhaps the accused sent it himself.'

'Hardly, sir, he's inside, though he's tried hard enough to get bail; two applications before the magistrate and one before the judge in chambers.' Sergeant Perry chuckled. 'Mr. Creedy, that's his solicitor, got really shirty when it was refused the last time.'

'Were you afraid he'd abscond?'

'One's afraid of everything where Mr. Creedy's clients are concerned. He's a bigger twister than most defending solicitors. Suppose I shouldn't say that to you, sir.'

'Oh I don't know, it'll be useful to bear in mind should you and I ever be on opposite sides.'

Sergeant Perry laughed uncertainly and Adam rang off. He read the letter through once more and then put it in his pocket. It seemed better not to leave it about, particularly as he had no intention of telling Charles Imrey of its existence.

A few minutes later Imrey came in and nonchalantly cast a large bundle of papers on to his desk.

'Still at it, Adam? I should think you must have learnt that brief by heart. Lucky chap to be able to give it so much time. Knowing Creedy, I don't expect I shall get a brief till five o'clock the day before the case comes on. Incidentally, if they want a conference you'll have to disappear.'

'You know I always do anyway when you have solicitors to see you', Adam replied, allowing himself to be nettled by Imrey's tone. 'And don't forget the same'll apply if I have a conference.'

'Well, try and fix one for when I'm out, otherwise it can be darned annoying.'

Imrey sat down and began to undo the piece of pink tape round a brief. Adam stared with dislike at the top of his head, deriving satisfaction from the increasing area of baldness he saw there. Satisfaction, since he knew that Charles Imrey was sensitive on the subject.

When he left chambers for the day, Adam made his way, as he often did, to a coffee-bar not far from the Temple. It was usually fairly empty at that hour, most home-goers preferring to stop, if anywhere, for refreshment of a sterner kind.

The youth behind the espresso machine nodded at Adam as he came in and handed him a large cup of black coffee. There were two girls sitting at one of the small tables, their heads almost touching in a whispered colloquy which was punctuated by giggles. At another table sat someone who could have been a barrister's clerk, except that one didn't usually find them in coffee-bars at a quarter past six of an evening. Alone at the counter, his back to Adam, was a young man deep in an evening paper.

Adam viewed them all without pleasure. Charles Imrey had the effect at times of turning him unreasonably against the whole human race.

He chose a stool at the counter and blew irritably at his cup of scalding coffee. It was quite unnecessary to serve it at the temperature of molten steel. He stretched for the sugar and knocked the arm of the young man two stools away. The young man turned to acknowledge his grunted apology and with a look of astonishment exclaimed, 'Good heavens, it's Adam.'

Adam's face broke into a smile of pleasure. 'Why, Tony, what are you doing here?'

'I've got to meet somebody in Fleet Street at half past six and came in here for a coffee as I was early. And you?'

'I work hereabouts.'

'Don't tell me you're a newspaperman?'

'No, not Fleet Street. The Temple.'

'A barrister?'

'Yes.'

There was silence while they grinningly appraised each other. Adam hadn't seen Tony Lelaker since they'd left school together seven years before. They had been exact contemporaries, having arrived as new boys in the same term and spending much of their school lives in one another's shadows. As a boy Tony Lelaker had been amusing, unprincipled, and wholly lacking in any respect for authority. He had come near to being expelled more than once, but Adam had never accorded him less than a grudging admiration.

'Yes, I remember now that you were destined for the Bar. Well, well.' Lelaker shook his head slowly as though finding it difficult to believe that Adam had really joined such eminent ranks. 'What sort of practice have you got, crime, divorce?'

'I think a general practice describes it best', Adam said dryly.

'A bit of everything, eh?'

'A very little of practically nothing, though today's been a red-letter one.' Lelaker listened while Adam told him about his case, his expression becoming positively eager at mention of the anonymous letter.

'You make me envious', he said a trifle wistfully, when Adam had finished. 'Compared with yours, my job completely lacks excitement.'

'What are you doing, Tony?'

'I'm in the property racket.'

'That spells money, doesn't it?'

'Mmm, it can do, though it's easier to lose a fortune than make one.'

'Nevertheless you're doing all right?'

'So far, though believe me, Adam, it's a rat race. Hard work, and if you're going to do any good, you've got to have a battle spirit allied to a gambler's instinct.'

'What's the name of the firm you work for?'

'I've got my own firm.' Noticing Adam's expression he went on, 'Only me and a luscious secretary and an office-boy.'

'I didn't think you'd be without an office-boy.' They laughed, for both knew that Tony Lelaker had been absorbed in the multiple attractions of the female sex since a more than usually early age. 'Incidentally, are you married, Tony?'

Lelaker shook his head. 'You?'

'No. Barristers can't support wives until they're almost too old to appreciate them.'

For the next ten minutes they reminisced about days not so very long past but sufficiently distant to seem to belong to another world.

'I must fly, Adam', Lelaker said looking at his watch. 'But give me a ring and come round for a drink one evening later this week. Bring this girl-friend of yours too. Sara, did you say her name was?'

Thus it was that three evenings later, Adam and Sara found themselves at Tony Lelaker's extremely comfortable flat near Marble Arch.

Adam gazed about him at the expensive fittings. 'The property business may lack excitement, but I can tell you that you'd need a good many briefs at the Bar to pay for this lot.' His eyes roamed round the room and came finally to rest on Sara, who signalled him a disapproving look. 'I can't help it, it's true', he replied aloud to her look.

'What's true?' Lelaker asked from the corner where he was mixing drinks.

'What I just said.'

'Yes, but think of the personal satisfaction you get out of your job, Adam. It has prestige, glamour . . .'

Adam made a rude noise.

Sara frowned again. For her the word 'barrister' connoted glamour and it upset her to hear Adam blow raspberries at his profession. Other young barristers she had met had invariably given the impression of belonging to an exclusive fraternity. But there! It was with Adam and not with any other young barrister that she was in love.

'You'll feel differently after this case of yours at the Old Bailey. That'll put you on the map', Lelaker said, coming across with a tray of gin and tonics. 'I can't wait to hear you in action, Adam.'

'Don't be silly, you're not coming.'

'Why not?'

Adam stared at the piece of lemon floating in his drink. 'Because it's going to be bad enough without having one's friends turning it into a human circus.'

'Nonsense.' Lelaker turned to Sara. 'Aren't you going to hear him, Sara?'

She looked hopefully towards Adam, but before she could answer, he'd said, 'No, she certainly isn't going to hear me.'

'Well, you won't keep me away so easily. If necessary, I shall say I'm a reporter covering the case for the old school magazine.'

It was at this moment that a door which Adam had thought must lead into a bedroom opened and a tarty-looking female came into the room. She appeared to be in the late twenties and had an extremely good figure and large, watchful eyes.

'Hi', she said to the room in general.

'Meet Debbie', Lelaker said, handing her the drink he'd just poured for himself and going off to get another.

'I've just been having a bath', Debbie announced, apparently to explain her absence from the room. Her eyes settled on Adam. 'Are you really a barrister? Tony's been telling me all about your case.'

21

'It seems there aren't many people who haven't heard about it one way or another.'

Debbie nodded gravely, ignoring his flippant tone, and an awkward silence fell. Adam could feel the faint waves of Sara's hostility radiating outwards from the sofa and wondered if they were equally obvious to the other two. He felt vaguely disgruntled and began to wish they hadn't come.

Tony Lelaker was an excellent host, however, with a stream of entertaining anecdotes about various deals and enterprises with which he had been concerned and soon Adam had forgotten his momentary irritation. It was clear that the years had served only to increase Lelaker's ingenuity and zest, and that maturity had done nothing to flatten his high spirits. Despite what he had said about his job lacking excitement, it seemed to Adam that some of the deals he talked about must have been anything but dull in their execution.

While Lelaker talked, he sat with an arm round Debbie's shoulder, occasionally caressing her neck or playing with the lobe of her ear. She appeared used to the treatment and sat with a mildly attentive expression on her face, though contributing nothing to the conversation apart from a small smile from time to time. Adam conjectured that not exactly being in the category of hostess or guest, she felt no obligation to play the part of either; or alternatively that her bath had made her sleepy and uncommunicative.

When he and Sara eventually got up to leave, she waved a tired hand in their direction and simply said, ''Bye.'

Lelaker saw them to the front door. 'I shall ring you next week, Adam, to find out about your case. I've always wanted to go to the Old Bailey and here's my chance. Besides, after that anonymous letter, you obviously ought to have a bodyguard and I'm just the fellow. I'll bring my sword-stick with me.'

'I don't want you there a bit', Adam retorted, though nevertheless flattered by the other's interest, and caught up once more in the spell of his infectious self-confidence.

'Sara wants me to protect you so there's my mandate', Lelaker said with mock solemnity.

A few minutes later, Adam and Sara were sauntering down Edgware Road.

'Enjoy yourself?' he asked.

'Yes; I liked Tony. I feel that he's someone who's really made a study of oneupmanship.'

'He was practising it in the pram. It's as natural to him as breathing. What did you think of Debbie?'

'I suppose she's his current mistress, isn't she?'

'Probably.'

She shot him a sidelong glance. 'If you really want to know, I think she looked a predatory bitch.'

Adam grinned.

'Apart from "hi" and "'bye" she scarcely spoke, so I don't see why you grade her quite so low.'

'Nevertheless that's what she is! Woman's instinct! However, I should think Tony's able to look after himself all right.'

'And me? Would I be able to?'

'You'd still be smiling oafishly as she gobbled you up.'

'Hey, Sara! That's not a very nice thing to say.'

She turned her head and gave him a quick butterfly kiss on the cheek. 'Darling', she murmured.

Adam's response was to pull her towards him and kiss her warmly on the lips.

'Hope William's not anywhere about', he said immediately afterwards. 'The idea of anyone from his chambers kissing a girl in public, and in Edgware Road of all streets, would give him a fatal seizure.'

As it was Friday evening they decided to surrender themselves to the dubious delights of a film at the local cinema near Sara's flat, followed by supper at a small Italian restaurant where the hardness of the cane-bottom chairs and the bareness of the décor were compensated for by mounds of simple, but delicious, food.

Saturday and Sunday passed equally pleasantly and it was with a distinct sense of melancholy that Adam walked back to his lodgings on Sunday night. What a contrast between this week-end and the last. Sara had been all gaiety, fun and sweet affection; Elsie Dunn had displayed neither gaiety nor fun, and her affection had been of the tail-wagging variety.

It was odd, he reflected as he undressed, that he had never tried to sleep with Sara, whom he liked much more than the few girls he had been to bed with. Could this be the writing on the wall – on the church wall?

As he climbed into bed, Adam wondered how he'd be feeling next Sunday night, for somehow the coming week promised change.

When he arrived at chambers the next morning, slightly earlier than usual, the first thing he saw on his desk was a letter. From the first quick glance he knew that it was *another* letter.

With a slightly trembling hand he opened it, recognizing the same schoolboy writing, the same mildly sinister blend of respect and menace.

He read :

'Dear Sir,

'I thought I'd just drop you another line to warn you again about believing Mrs. Young's evidence. She's lying and it wouldn't do for you to press the case to the jury. The best thing would be to drop the charge. As before, I'm afraid I must remain anonymous, but please don't let that fact make you disregard my advice.'

He wondered whether he should phone Detective-Sergeant Perry, but with memories of their previous conversation decided not to. He'd hand it to him when they met at court. The last thing he wanted was for the patronizing Sergeant to think the letter had upset him. It hadn't and a few days' delay wouldn't make any difference.

And in this, he was perfectly right.

CHAPTER THREE

IT WAS around tea-time the following afternoon that William came in to Adam's and Charles Imrey's room, and said, 'Young is in the list tomorrow, following a part heard in court six.'

'Tch!' Imrey tossed his head impatiently. 'I was hoping it wouldn't come on till next week, I've got that awkward Rent Act case the day after tomorrow. Think you'll be able to fix things, William?'

William, whose life was made up of arranging for one person to be as nearly as possible in two places at the same time, nodded unconcernedly.

'Suppose it doesn't worry you?' Imrey went on, casting an eye over Adam's near briefless table.

'Suits me rather well as a matter of fact', Adam replied in a casual tone. 'I'd like to get it over this week.'

'Oh well, tomorrow we battle.'

Although Imrey had had a lengthy conference about the case with his instructing solicitor, he had dropped no hints about his defence nor indeed ever referred to the case since he'd learnt Adam was prosecuting. Adam for his part had similarly refrained from mentioning it, if only to preserve himself from a snub. Moreover, he was prepared to guess that Imrey had deliberately behaved in this way as part of a war of nerves before they reached the actual battlefield.

Adam took his brief home that evening and re-read it after supper, sitting on the edge of his bed. By now, he really did know it by heart and would not be embarrassed should he leave it on a bus the next morning.

The butterflies which normally took possession of his stomach on the mornings he was due to appear in court, this time turned up on the evening before and gave him a disturbed night.

The next morning he gave his hair an extra good brush, though seeing that it was to be covered by a wig, it was perhaps less necessary than usual. This, however, did not occur to him at the time, as he peered at his set expression in the mirror.

After breakfast the butterflies multiplied and he tried to concentrate his mind on worse ordeals than the one which lay ahead. Saint Sebastian and those gruesome arrows for example; or Edward II and the red-hot poker; even Adam Cape, a desperately homesick nine-year-old, far from home, facing his first day at boarding-school in England.

'Good luck with your case, Mr. Cape', Miss Brown called out as Adam passed her door.

'Thanks, Miss B.'

She was a kindly soul even if she was versed in every conceivable form of boarding-house stinginess.

When Adam arrived at the Old Bailey he saw that the presiding judge of Court 6 was Mr. Commissioner Arthurson, Q.C., who was not one of the permanent judges of the court but an elderly member of the Bar who had retired from practice and who was frequently pressed into part-time judicial service. He had a reputation for being laconic and aloof and he looked not unlike a well-bred horse.

By the time Adam had put on his robes and taken himself off to Court 6, it was nearly half past ten. Promptly at the half-hour, the judge took his seat and began summing-up the case which had been adjourned from the previous day.

Adam slipped into a seat beside the counsel who was prosecuting in the case.

'How long do you reckon?'

'You in the next case?'

'Yes.'

'Shouldn't think his summing-up will occupy more than half an hour or so.'

Adam idly turned the pages of an album of photographs which were on the ledge in front of him. They showed the corner of a field surrounded by a high hedge and bushes.

'Typical piece of rape country, isn't it?' his neighbour remarked.

'That the charge?'

'What else?'

Adam felt someone give his gown a tug and turned to find an eager face bent towards him.

'Mr. Cape? I'm Detective-Sergeant Perry. Can I have a word with you outside, sir?'

Adam extricated himself, unaware of the peevish eye cast in his direction by the judge.

'Would you like to have a word with the wife before the case comes on, sir?'

Adam shook his head. 'I don't think that would be advisable. The defence might try and suggest something.'

'As you like, sir', Sergeant Perry replied in a slightly huffed tone. 'I just thought it might help to put her at her ease. She's a mass of nerves this morning.'

'But she'll come up to proof all right, won't she?' Adam asked anxiously. The prospect of his chief witness crumbling was not a reassuring one.

'I've coached her all right,' Sergeant Perry said with more truth than discretion, 'it's just that she's in the hell of a mess.'

'Did you have trouble getting her to court?'

'No, she came without any bother, but she's just like a jelly that's been left out in the sun.'

Adam swallowed uncomfortably. 'By the way, I had another anonymous letter.'

He handed it to Sergeant Perry, who read it through with a portentous air and said, 'Not much hope of tracing the fellow who wrote it, sir. At least not at this juncture.'

Adam was about to ask what exactly he meant when Charles Imrey came hurrying up. He wore his wig and gown with the same natural ease he did his shirt and trousers and said importantly, 'I gather we'll be on in about five minutes.' He passed into court carrying several large tomes under his arm.

A further shot in the war of nerves, Adam told himself. There was scarcely a fragment of law in the whole case, certainly nothing which required volumes of law reports.

With the butterflies now more or less under control, Adam pushed his way back into court to await events.

The judge was in the final sentence of his summing-up and as soon as the jury had retired, the rapist and Frankie Young swapped over places, a new jury was sworn and the trial was under way.

Adam rose to his feet and, in a voice which sounded to him little like his own, began his opening address.

'May it please your lordship, members of the jury, the accused who is charged . . .'

'I appear to defend in this case, my lord', Charles Imrey broke in imperiously and added in an aside to Adam, 'It's usual for prosecuting counsel to make the introductions.'

For a second Adam felt ashamed, then merely annoyed by the gratuitous interruption. 'As I was about to tell you, members of the jury, the accused, who is charged with the offence known to the law as wounding with intent, is defended by my learned friend Mr. Imrey, while I appear on behalf of the prosecution.' He paused long enough to cast a 'so there' look at Imrey and went on, 'The facts of the case are straightforward and are contained almost wholly in the evidence of the accused's wife who was the victim of this attack and who will tell you . . .' Here, Adam proceeded to tell the jury what, he hoped, Carole Young would say when she reached the witness-box. At all events it was what she had said in the Magistrates' Court. He then dealt with the rest of the evidence and concluded, 'And so, members of the jury, the prosecution allege that there isn't the slightest doubt that this man deliberately attacked his wife with this sharp knife and . . .'

Charles Imrey interrupted again, this time in an unpleasantly silky tone.

'I don't see how my learned friend can say there isn't "the slightest doubt" before the evidence has even been called.'

'I think,' said the judge with a sniff, 'that what Mr. Cape means is that the jury should not have the slightest doubt about the case when they've heard the evidence.'

'It's not what he said, my lord, and it struck me as an

30

unfortunate form of words to be used in an opening, but I don't wish to make an issue of it.'

Imrey sat down and tapped his teeth with a pencil; and the judge gazing dispassionately at Adam said, 'Go on, Mr. Cape.'

'Thank you, my lord. As I was saying, members of the jury, the prosecution will invite you to say when you've heard all the evidence that this charge has been proved beyond a reasonable doubt.' He sat down and wiped a hand across his forehead which was covered with beads of perspiration. But his opening was over and he felt a sudden upsurge of confidence.

While the judge held a whispered conversation with the clerk of the court, Adam took the opportunity of studying the man in the dock.

Frankie Young looked somewhere in the late twenties. He had a thin pointed nose, a weak chin and brown hair brushed neatly back. There was a pallor about his skin which was accentuated by the isolated spots of colour around his cheek-bones. The shiftless nature of his character apparent in his looks was confirmed by the existence of his previous convictions. One for larceny, one for obtaining credit by fraud and one for loitering with intent to commit a felony. For the last mentioned, he had served fifteen months. His first two convictions had not earned him prison sentences.

The seats at the side of the dock and behind it were filled and Adam caught sudden sight of Tony Lelaker sitting in a row normally reserved for more important visitors. Trust Tony!

There was a further delay while the jury in the previous

case returned to court to give their verdict and then Mr. Commissioner Arthurson said wearily, 'Yes, yes, Mr. Cape, now let's get on.'

The first witness was Carole Young. She was dressed in a simple cotton frock, over which she wore an unbuttoned raincoat. Her hair, which was dark, reached to her shoulders but it was her expression which Adam at once noticed. She was plain scared. It showed in her eyes and was reflected in her voice as she took the oath.

'Is your name Carole Young?' Adam began, accompanying the question with a comforting smile.

'Yes.'

'And do you live at 38 Warren Place, N.22?'

'Yes.'

Her voice was scarcely above a whisper and with a weary sigh the judge laid down his pencil and prepared to deliver one of his well-worn homilies.

'Madam, if your evidence is to be of the slightest value you'll have to speak much louder than that.' He raised his own voice. 'As loud as this if you like. There is nothing more exasperating to a jury, or to a judge for that matter, than to have to strain their ears in order to hear what a witness is saying.' Carole Young watched him as though he were some great bird about to swoop at her. 'So please speak up, madam.'

'And is the accused your husband?'

'Yes.'

'Louder', cried the judge.

'Yes.'

'Have you any children?'

'One, a baby girl.'

'Mrs. Young, I want to ask you some questions about what happened on the evening of Friday the fourteenth of June.' The witness looked blank and Adam hurriedly added, 'That was the evening the assault took place.'

'I had thought it was the witness who was supposed to be giving evidence', Imrey broke in. 'Not counsel for the prosecution.'

'I'm just directing the witness's mind to the particular event, as I'm entitled to', Adam retorted with some heat.

'Yes, that was not a necessary interruption, Mr. Imrey', the judge whinnied, glaring all round the court.

'What happened that evening, Mrs. Young?'

Carole Young took a quick look at her husband in the dock and then gripping the ledge of the witness-box once more retailed her evidence, prompted only occasionally by questions from Adam. It came out with anguish, with difficulty, but also with an air of inevitability that quite moved Adam. As he listened, he realized how much she still loved her husband despite what he had done to her, and when, his examination-in-chief completed, he resumed his seat, his sympathy went out to her as Charles Imrey rose to cross-examine.

For a few silent seconds, Imrey just stared at her coldly, before hurling his first hectoring question. 'You're lying, aren't you? You've told lie after lie, haven't you?'

The girl shook her head in mute anguish.

'It isn't true that your husband attacked you, is it?'

'Yes.'

'The truth is that you got hysterical and picked up the knife and got injured when he was trying to wrest it from you, isn't it?'

33

'No.'

'What did happen then?'

'What I said. He picked up the knife and stabbed me.' Her voice had once more dropped to a mere whisper, but there was now a reek of drama as distinct as the acrid smell of cordite after an explosion.

Adam bit anxiously at the skin round his thumb-nail, wondering what he could do to try and lessen her ordeal.

'He picked up the knife and stabbed you, did he?' Imrey's tone was scornful. 'Your evidence is improving all the time, isn't it, Mrs. Young?' She looked at him in bewilderment. 'What you said in answer to my learned friend's question was that he picked up the knife, came towards you and *the next thing you knew was a sharp pain in your shoulder.* That's quite different, isn't it, from what you're now saying?'

'I don't know.'

'Well, the jury will.'

Adam rose. 'I don't think my friend has any right to make such a comment.'

'Nor do I', the judge agreed readily. 'Kindly confine yourself to questions, Mr. Imrey.'

Charles Imrey accepted the reproof with disdain.

'Do you agree, Mrs. Young, that this is the first time you've ever said your husband stabbed you?'

'Mr. Imrey,' the judge broke in, 'she mayn't have stated it in terms before but it was the clear inference to be drawn from her evidence. The trouble is that you've now got her completely confused.'

'I'm sorry, my lord, if you think I'm deliberately trying to confuse the witness.'

Mr. Commissioner Arthurson ignored him and turning to the witness said, 'Did you, or did you not, madam, actually see your husband stab you?'

'No.'

'And in whose hand was the knife immediately before you felt the pain in your shoulder?'

'His.'

'Liar!' Young had started out of his chair in the dock and was being restrained by two warders.

'Yes, continue your cross-examination, Mr. Imrey', the judge said when order had been restored.

But Charles Imrey had been put out of his stride and the remainder of his cross-examination consisted in putting his client's version of events to the witness and having it denied on all the essentials.

Adam being uncertain what he should ask in re-examination decided to stay silent, and Carole Young left the witness-box.

The remaining three witnesses occupied little time and only an hour and a quarter after Adam had first stood up to open the case, he announced, 'That is the case for the prosecution, my lord.'

Though it had been far plainer sailing than he had anticipated, he nevertheless had the sensation of having spent the time in violent and unaccustomed physical exercise. He was stiff and aching all over, but as Imrey in turn announced that he would call the prisoner and Adam watched Young leave the dock and make his way to the witness-box, he realized there were several laps yet to come.

Charles Imrey turned a page of his brief and adopting a

solemn air said, 'You've heard your wife give evidence. Is what she told the court true?'

'No.'

'What isn't true?'

'That I had the knife and stabbed her.'

'What did happen?'

'She picked up the knife and stabbed herself.'

Mr. Commissioner Arthurson looked up sharply, like a horse about to neigh.

'Stabbed herself?' he asked.

'Well, sort of.'

'If he may amplify his answer, my lord', Charles Imrey said anxiously.

'I think he'd better.'

'How did your wife come to stab herself, Young?'

'Well, she picked up this knife and I thought she was going to stab herself so I went to take it from her and as I got hold of her wrist, well, it just happened.'

'What just happened?'

'She got injured.'

'In whose hand was the knife at the time?'

'Hers.'

'She says it was in yours?'

'She's lying.'

'Did you cause her to stab herself?'

Young wiped a hand across his mouth, as he glared about him. 'Course I didn't. I got hold of her wrist and then she let out a cry that she'd been stabbed. She must either have done it herself or it was an accident.'

Imrey nodded sagaciously and turned over another page of his brief. Then he bent down and whispered to Mr.

Creedy, his instructing solicitor, who was sitting immediately in front of him.

When he stood up again, he folded his arms across his chest and in a measured drawl asked, 'Did you have any reason to stab your wife?'

'No.'

'Does she have any reason to say you did?'

'Yes.'

'What?'

'Revenge.'

'For what?'

'I'd rather not say.' Young stared stolidly at the opposite wall, aware that he had become the focus of fresh attention.

'You must, Young. The jury want to know', Charles Imrey said firmly.

The prisoner wiped the back of his hand across his mouth again and looked ill at ease.

'Because . . . because she was jealous over my going out with another woman.'

There was an anguished 'Oh!' from where Carole Young was sitting at the back of the court and her husband threw a vindictive glance in her direction. Wrapping his gown about him, Charles Imrey sat down, casting a not very different sort of look in Adam's direction.

The judge peered thoughtfully at counsel and said, 'Mr. Imrey, that was never put to Mrs. Young in cross-examination.'

'I'm sorry, my lord.'

'I shall, of course, have to draw the jury's attention to the significance of that.' Charles Imrey made no reply. 'The court will now adjourn until five minutes past two.'

As Adam made his way out of court he saw a tall young man, whom he had noticed sitting at the back, engage Mr. Creedy in earnest conversation.

'You were terrific, Adam.' Tony Lelaker had pushed his way to Adam's side and was beaming enthusiastically.

Adam grinned sheepishly. 'What impression did you form?'

'Of you?'

'No, of the case.'

'He'll be acquitted, won't he?'

'I hope not.'

'But I mean it's word against word, so surely the jury's bound to give him the benefit of the doubt. Isn't that the way it works?'

'No, it isn't', Adam said coldly. 'If they believe her and not him, no benefit of the doubt enters into it, they should convict.'

'Well, come and have a spot of lunch anyway.'

As they emerged from court, Adam noticed Carole Young standing by herself looking infinitely forlorn. He gave her a smile which she returned with a watery one of her own.

'You look far better in a wig than I imagined you would', Lelaker went on brightly. 'You must have the right shaped head.'

'Simply that I haven't had my hair cut recently. When I've been shorn, it's apt to slip over my ears and look as though a rice pudding has been spilt over my head.'

Adam would much rather have had a quick meal on his own and have spent a quiet time mentally preparing his cross-examination of Young, but Lelaker swept him across the road to a public house and put half a pint of beer in his hand before he had any opportunity to demur. And then it was too late.

By the time he returned to court after lunch, he was regretting the occasion more than ever, since his friend had considerably depressed him with his bland certainty that Young was going to be acquitted.

'Are you really coming back this afternoon?' Adam had asked when he had finally torn himself away to go and robe.

'Of course I am. It's fascinating and I must hear the result. Besides, don't forget, that anonymous letter-writer may be lurking around!'

As Adam was about to go back into court, Detective-Sergeant Perry came up to him.

'Going to pot him all right, sir?'

Adam shrugged his shoulders.

'I hope so.'

'I hope so too. He ought to get at least eighteen months. You'll make mincemeat of him in your cross-examination.'

Adam gave him a thin and unenthusiastic smile and went into court. As he pushed past Charles Imrey, the latter said, 'You've lost this case, Adam, the jury'll never convict on that woman's evidence.' Mr. Creedy smiled approvingly, revealing an uneven row of yellow teeth.

Adam resumed his seat, wishing the day was more than half-way through.

A few minutes later, Mr. Commissioner Arthurson took his place on the bench and invited Adam to begin his cross-examination.

As he rose to his feet and stared at Young across the divide of the court in what seemed an eternity of silence, he endeavoured to remember all he had ever learnt about the art of cross-examination. Books and colleagues had always been full of advice on the subject.

To cross-examine does not mean to ask questions crossly, the books were fond of reminding the tyro. And again, don't, it was rubbed in, ask the witness the same questions his own counsel has just asked. Similarly, don't repeat the witness's evidence back to him by prefacing it with, 'Are you *really* saying . . .?' And if the witness has categorically stated that he did not have an egg for his breakfast, there's nothing to be gained by glaring at him and barking, 'I put it to you that you did. . . .'

All were excellent precepts, but they left Adam standing in court without a question to ask.

'Yes, Mr. Cape', the judge urged when the silence had become noticeable.

Adam swallowed hard. 'Are you really saying that your wife stabbed herself?'

'She must have done, mustn't she?'

'Why?'

''Cause I didn't.'

'But it doesn't follow that . . .' His words trailed away as yet another 'don't' entered his mind. Don't get drawn into an argument with the witness. 'Why should she make this charge against you if it isn't true?'

''Cause of what I said. Out of jealousy.'

'It was pretty drastic action to take?'

'You're telling me.'

Adam frowned. It was being even more difficult than he had feared. 'Do you really think a woman would try and get her husband put into prison simply because she was jealous of his going out with another woman?'

Charles Imrey sprang up. 'I suggest, my lord, that's hardly a question the witness can answer. It's an invitation to speculation.'

'Reframe your question, Mr. Cape.'

'Do you really believe that your wife is trying to get you into prison?'

Once more Imrey was on his feet.

'I object to that question, too, my lord. It's not for the witness to express an opinion on his wife's intentions.'

'I agree.' Mr. Commissioner Arthurson peered at Adam over the top of his spectacles. 'Try and frame your questions more precisely, Mr. Cape.'

But by now Adam felt as though he had been caught up in a tide of thick treacle, and decided to conclude his cross-examination with as little loss of face as possible. With a growing sense of futility, he embarked on a series of questions which Young proceeded to counter with flat contradictions. Hardly listening to the answers he thrust on to the end.

'I put it to you, Young, that you deliberately stabbed your wife. . . .'

'I didn't.'

'. . . And that *your* version of what happened is quite untrue?'

'It isn't.'

Adam sat thankfully down.

'No re-examination, my lord', Charles Imrey announced in a tone which rang with confidence. 'And that is the defendant's case, my lord.'

'Yes, Mr. Cape, you wish to address the jury?'

Once more he was on his feet. This was his last chance to remedy the débacle of his inept cross-examination and he

41

mustn't waste it. If he made a mess of this too, then he might as well quit the law this very afternoon. That, at any rate, was how he felt as he began his final speech.

To describe it as a *tour de force* would be an exaggeration, but the fact was that desperation appeared to lend wings to his words with the result that he presented an eloquent and well-marshalled argument for a conviction, which was the more effective for being short. It even had Charles Imrey listening attentively and making rapid notes.

'Thank you, Mr. Cape.' The judge said in a not un-friendly tone as Adam sat down.

Imrey's own final speech was longer and a much more ponderous piece of advocacy, but nevertheless put across with persuasive power.

The judge's summing-up was short and not particularly helpful. It was almost as if he hadn't made up his own mind which side to believe. In the end, almost every view he expressed was cancelled out by the next and he constantly reminded the jury, 'It's entirely a matter for you.'

The jury retired and Adam went outside into the corridor for a smoke. Tony Lelaker joined him there.

'That was a fiery speech you made, Adam', he said with a short laugh. 'Didn't know you could be so vehement.'

'Still think he'll get off?'

'All I can say is that he would if I were on the jury.'

'Then I'm glad you're not.'

Lelaker looked at him with a faint frown.

'I thought prosecuting counsel weren't supposed to be wildly partisan these days.'

'I'm not, but I happen to think this is a true bill and I wouldn't like him to get off through any failure on my part.'

Charles Imrey was pacing up and down the corridor talking to Mr. Creedy while Sergeant Perry was over in a corner deep in conversation with Carole Young.

Tony Lelaker had become oddly abstracted and when he had finished his cigarette Adam wandered back into court.

It's an enervating experience waiting for a jury to reach their verdict, not unlike that of waiting to board an aeroplane whose departure has been indefinitely delayed.

But suddenly in a mysterious way everybody seemed to know that the jury was ready to come back. The court refilled and an expectant hush fell as the judge took his seat.

The Clerk of the Court rose.

'Members of the jury, are you agreed upon your verdict?'

'We are.'

'Do you find the prisoner guilty or not guilty?'

The foreman appeared to study a piece of paper in his hand.

'Not guilty', he declared, and looked a trifle anxiously at the judge.

'I ask that the prisoner be discharged, my lord', Charles Imrey said in a ringing tone.

'Yes.' Then turning to the jury, Mr. Commissioner Arthurson said reassuringly, 'I may say that I agree entirely with your verdict.'

Adam shot him a look of disgust. There was no need for the judge to ally himself publicly with a verdict which Adam himself thought perverse.

Bundling his papers under his arm, Adam pushed his way out of court and headed for the robing-room. He had no wish to speak to anyone and was thankful that Tony Lelaker was nowhere in sight.

A slight tug at his gown caused him to look round, however.

'May I speak to you a moment, sir?' Carole Young was looking at him pleadingly. *'Please,* sir.'

Adam received a sharp shove from behind.

'I'm most terribly sorry, but someone pushed into me.' It was the tall young man whom he had earlier seen talking to Mr. Creedy. He accepted the apology with a grunt and turned back to Carole Young who appeared to be on the verge of tears.

'I must talk to someone. . . .'

She twisted the handle of her handbag in anguish as she waited, a forlorn and lonely figure 'midst a scurrying throng.

Adam felt acutely embarrassed. Why must she pick on him? He had merely been hired to present a case in court, not get emotionally embroiled with witnesses out of court.

'Look, Mrs. Young, I'm afraid there's nothing I can do for you. Have a word with Detective-Sergeant Perry.'

She made no reply, but looked at him with desperate eyes as he turned and walked off down the corridor, more disturbed by the encounter than he cared to admit.

Lelaker now loomed up in his path. 'Hello, Adam, I must fly. Got to have my hair cut before the barber closes. It's been a fascinating day and you were terrific. Glad I shan't be called upon to protect you, though, from your anonymous correspondent. We must meet again soon. I'll phone you.' With a wave of the hand, he ran down the stairs and was gone.

Adam made his way to the robing-room, hoping that Charles Imrey would already have left. But he hadn't.

44

'Ah, there you are, Adam', he said, with a smirk. 'Going back to chambers?'

Though it had been his intention to do so, Adam now said, 'No.'

''Fraid I must. Got to pick up some papers for tomorrow. I'm first in the list at Maidstone Quarter Sessions.' He walked across to a mirror and, removing his bands, put his tie on. 'Saw you talking to your chief witness outside court, what's she think of the result?'

'What would you, if you were in her shoes, poor soul?' Adam retorted bitterly.

Imrey shrugged his shoulders. 'Depends on whether I'd told the truth or not.'

'Well, now it's all over, where *do* you think the truth lay?'

'My dear Adam, I don't know and I don't particularly care.' He turned and fixed Adam with a sardonic eye. 'And take a tip from me, don't start identifying yourself with your client's case or you might as well give up trying to be an advocate. And anyway, as far as those two are concerned, they're probably back in each other's arms by now.'

Adam turned away and taking off his wig returned it to its metal box. He knew there was sound sense in what Imrey had just said, but he recoiled from the cynical indifference of his tone. Imrey now went on, 'If it's any help to your conscience, and for what it's worth, Creedy's been convinced all along that the wife was lying.'

'Sergeant Perry felt the opposite.'

'Oh, well, if you're always going to believe everything the police tell you about a case, you're really sticking your head in the sand.'

'And Creedy? Why should one accept his word?'

Charles Imrey shook his head slowly from side to side and said in a tone of weary patience, 'You don't have to accept Creedy's word about anything. Forget that I ever mentioned it. I only did so as it seemed it might provide a bit of balm to your apparently raw feelings about the case.' He picked up his things and prepared to go. 'However, don't feel too badly, that final speech of yours was a jolly good one.'

Adam's jaw dropped in surprise. A word of praise from Charles Imrey was the last thing he had expected, but Imrey didn't wait for his reaction.

After leaving the Old Bailey, Adam went into a call-box and phoned Sara. He had no desire to talk to her about the case at that moment, but she had extracted a promise from him that he would do so as soon as it was over. He hoped she wouldn't overdo the sympathy and to his relief she didn't.

'What are you doing this evening?' she asked when he had given her the bare report.

'I've got some letters to write. Haven't written to the family for three weeks, so I'd better put that right.'

Though obviously disappointed, she didn't attempt to dissuade him and for this he was also grateful. The truth was that she was beginning not only to recognize his moods, but to know how to handle them.

When he had rung off, he caught a bus into the West End and walked through Berkeley Square to the pool he always went to for a swim.

For once, however, the clear, chemical water failed in its magic and, concentrate though he would on the sheer physical movement of his body, he couldn't get Carole Young's face out of his mind. 'I must talk to someone. . . .'

But why had she approached him? Presumably only because he had smiled at her in court and had looked and sounded kind. Why else! And why had he done that? Was it because he had been sorry for her and did wish to be kind, or had it simply been to ease his own task in eliciting her evidence? Whichever it was, Adam reflected grimly, *she* had clearly assumed it to be the former. She took him for a kind person who would help her. And what had he done but brush her aside and walk away in embarrassment? But what else could he have done? Barristers shouldn't get involved in the personal troubles of their witnesses, Charles Imrey had been quite right about that. No, he'd done all he should, he'd told her to speak to the police. To Sergeant Perry! Well, it wasn't Adam's fault that he was the officer in charge of the case.

When he left the swimming-pool he went and had a light meal and then realizing that letter-writing was out of the question in his present self-accusatory mood, decided he'd best round off the day by escaping into a cinema. From the huge picture outside, the film at the London Pavilion looked as though it ought to distract his mind for an hour or two.

But as Adam watched an ungainly monster from outer space snatching up pretty girls in summer frocks, he was suddenly aware that each had the face of Carole Young, and by the time he came out he had made up his mind.

Taking a Piccadilly Line train north, he travelled as far as Finsbury Park and then asked the way to Warren Place. A threepenny bus ride brought him to within short walking distance.

Number 38 was nearer the other end.

Now that he'd actually arrived in the street where the

47

Youngs lived, he thought he must be mad to have come and very nearly turned back and went home.

It was just before ten o'clock and daylight had given way prematurely to the gloomy dusk of a wet summer evening as he walked slowly along the street in a sort of wild dream.

The houses on each side had seen better days and appeared now to be mostly let off in rooms or 'Bed and Breakfast Apartments' as cards in some of the front windows more pretentiously advertised.

Number 38 was four houses from the end and Adam viewed it with misgiving from the opposite side of the street, to which he had purposely crossed. What on earth had induced him to come on such a ridiculous errand! Even now he'd much better turn round and go home to Kensington. What on earth would William think if he ever knew that one of the members of his chambers had acted with such an impulsive disregard of etiquette? Worse still, what a field-day Charles Imrey would have spreading the news of Adam's amusingly quixotic behaviour.

'Can I help you?'

Adam started guiltily and turned to find a tall, thin man who was wearing a scruffy raincoat and a check cap standing behind him. In one hand the man held a dog-lead at which a small mongrel dog was tugging furiously, but he was taking no notice of the animal and just stared at Adam from deep-sunk eyes.

'Oh, er, I . . . I . . . actually I was looking for a Mrs. Young.'

'I seem to know the name', the man said, without removing his eyes from Adam's face.

'I believe she lives at number 38.'

'That's number 38 over there.' The man pointed across the street in the direction in which Adam had been gazing before he came up.

'Oh, yes . . . er, thank you.'

There was now nothing for it but to go over and at least make a pretence of looking for someone.

The door of number 38 was ajar and Adam gingerly pushed it open. A naked bulb lit the bare hall in which a bicycle and a baby's pram were parked. A few yards along on the left there was a door with a piece of card pinned to it, but not a sound of movement came from anywhere inside the house.

Adam moved two cautious paces forward to look at the card on the door. 'Mr. and Mrs. Young' it said in faded ink.

Wondering what on earth he was going to say when someone answered, he knocked quietly on the door. But nobody did answer and after a brief second of indecision he tried the handle. The door opened and he found himself looking into a poorly-furnished room partitioned by a curtain which hung precariously from a thin rod suspended between two walls. On the other side of the curtain he could see a divan bed on which the bedclothes had been pulled up with little attempt at tidying.

Though the light was on, a glance told him that there was no one in the room. In one corner there was a gas-ring with a saucepan on it and in another an old-fashioned wash-jug and basin.

His attention was caught by a piece of paper which was on the table in the centre of the room, a table which was otherwise bare, apart from a plant in a pot.

He felt as he had done once at school, when, on being

summoned to the headmaster's study, he had found the room empty and had taken the opportunity of making a stealthy reconnaissance of this holy of holies.

He quietly closed the door behind him before moving over to the table.

His heart was now knocking hard against his chest wall and both his aural and visual senses were almost agonizingly alert.

The note on the table, which was typewritten, bore quite a short message, which read :

'Meet me under the canal bridge at the end of Mulhouse Street at ten o'clock this evening and I'll do my best to help you.'

As his eyes reached the end, Adam suddenly felt the blood drain from his head and an awful sweat break out over his body.

For the note was signed 'Adam Cape'.

CHAPTER FOUR

IT WAS like a nightmare. Though he was seized with blind panic, he could only stand staring, mesmerized by the note. Who had written it and why had they used his name? The question spun endlessly round his head without getting an answer. A minute ago he had been Adam Cape, a relatively carefree young man, now with shattering suddenness his world had tilted off its axis, sending him whirling through space, powerless and scared.

It seemed that hours went by before he regained control of his senses, though in fact it was something less than a minute.

Though still a considerably frightened young man, the instinct of self-preservation came to his rescue and his one idea was to get far away from the house as quickly as possible.

A sound of movement in the passage outside caught his ear and without conscious thought he dived behind the curtain which partitioned the room.

The next moment the door opened and someone came in.

As he cowered between a chair and dressing-table he thought that his legs must give way or that his breathing, which to his own ears sounded like a steam locomotive thundering through a tunnel, must attract attention.

Neither happened, however, and after only a few seconds

he heard the door open and close again. It was some time, however, before he felt sufficiently composed to emerge from his hiding-place.

Silence still reigned throughout the house as he tiptoed across the room towards the door. Then he suddenly noticed. The note had gone. A faint aura of perfume lingered in its place.

Carole Young must have come back for it, and now she had gone off to meet the mysterious stranger who had written to her in Adam's name.

It wasn't until he had put a hundred yards between himself and the house that he slowed down to consider his next move.

Two possibilities came to mind. One was to continue on home, the other to go resolutely to the canal bridge and find out exactly what was going on.

Adam's mind never wavered as to which he would do, however, and it was with a sigh of relief that he reached the tube station and thankfully boarded the first train headed in the direction of home.

CHAPTER FIVE

A<small>RE</small> <small>YOU</small> feeling all right this morning, Mr. Cape?'
William asked when Adam arrived in chambers the
next day.

'Yes', he replied as casually as he could in the hope of
forestalling further inquiry into his health.

That he felt anything but all right was primarily due to
lack of sleep. His eyes were red-rimmed and he had cut his
chin shaving.

'I'm afraid I wasn't in court for your final speech to the
jury yesterday afternoon, but I hear it was a most effective
one.'

'Yes; so effective the chap was acquitted.'

William frowned at the facetious retort and said primly,
'Good advocacy doesn't always get the results it deserves.
Anyway the Yard were pleased with the way you did the
case which is what matters.'

Adam accepted the tribute with scepticism, and in any
event, as he felt at the moment, the Yard's enthusiasm for
him, other than as a criminal, might prove to be short-lived.

'Are you quite sure you're feeling all right, sir?'

'I didn't sleep very well. Otherwise I'm all right.'

The telephone in the clerk's office began to ring and
William turned to answer it. 'There's a careless driving on
your table. Hendon Magistrates' Court next Friday.'

'Defence?'

'Yes.'

He was thankful that Charles Imrey was out and that he would therefore have their room to himself for the morning.

For some minutes he sat staring blankly at the wall in front of him, his thoughts once more chasing each other in an ever tight circle.

With a frustrated groan, he picked up the brief which William had left on his table and began to read it. But it was no good, his mind was in no mood to absorb the dreary details of a piece of bad driving on the North Circular. And when, three times without a glimmer of comprehension, he had read through his client's proof of evidence explaining inadequately but at length how he had come to run into the back of a bus at the traffic lights, he pushed the papers to one side and with sudden resolution put a call through to Detective-Sergeant Perry.

'Yes, sir, what can I do for you?' Sergeant Perry asked briskly when he had announced himself.

Adam's discomfiture grew. Why hadn't he paused to consider exactly what he was going to say? What he wanted to find out was clear enough, but what would the officer think if he said boldly, 'I was only ringing up to ask how things are with the Youngs today.'

'Did Mrs. Young speak to you as you were leaving court yesterday evening, Sergeant?'

'No, sir, not that I recall. In fact, I know I didn't see her after the case at all.' He paused. 'Was there any special reason for your asking, sir?'

'Actually, she tried to speak to me and I told her to see you.'

'Well, she didn't. What was it about, anyway?'

'I don't know, though she did say it was important and I thought she seemed anxious.'

'Probably was. Worried her husband might take it out of her.' Sergeant Perry laughed mirthlessly. 'I'd like to knock both their heads together.'

'You haven't had any news of her since the case? I mean you haven't been round to their house or anything?'

'No, not a peep out of either of them, but we shall have soon enough if trouble breaks out again. Don't you worry about that pair, sir. He was lucky to get away with it, but domestic fracas are commonplace round these parts, and more often than not they don't get to court. Ranks are closed before a policeman ever arrives on the doorstep. No, you take my advice, sir, and forget about them.'

Adam murmured his thanks, apologized for having disturbed him and rang off. Though the call had not been entirely satisfactory, it was reassuring to know that all was apparently quiet in Warren Place.

Sergeant Perry at his end of the line replaced the telephone receiver and looking across at his room-mate said derisively, 'Honestly! Some of these young barristers almost want you to change their nappies. That Cape we had in the Young case is worrying about what's going to happen to Mrs. Young now her husband's out and about. Seems to think I've got nothing better to do than sit around and pat her hand all day.'

The officer to whom these observations were addressed grunted sympathetically without looking up from the report of an attempted bank robbery he was drafting.

'Suppose he'll grow out of it', Sergeant Perry went on.

'He ought to spend a week here, that'd soon clear his system of sentimental slush.'

Adam, meanwhile, was busily building up the reassurance which the aftermath of his telephone call had brought him. If anything awful had happened to Carole Young, Sergeant Perry would have known. It was beginning to look as though it might have been her husband who had sent the note. Perhaps he had feared to come straight home and had known she mightn't respond to a note signed in his own name. He would have seen in court how Adam had gained his wife's confidence, so what better than to use his name to lure her out of the house. LURE, that word had an ominous ring and was it really likely that Frankie Young *would* have resorted to such a subterfuge to see his wife?

Happily, before Adam's spirits could drop again, the phone rang and he heard Tony Lelaker's voice.

'Sorry I had to dash away in such a hurry yesterday afternoon, Adam. But it was nice of you to let me come and hear you in action. It was an enthralling day.'

'No need to be so smooth. You know quite well that if I could have stopped your coming, I should have.'

Lelaker laughed. 'You're too modest. What's more you're obviously in the right job. I only hope that by the time my past catches up with me, you'll be on the Bench. I'll put on the old school tie to soften your heart.'

'It'll be ten years whatever you've done.'

Lelaker laughed again. He sounded in high spirits. 'Anyway, how are things today? No repercussions?'

'What do you mean?' Adam asked in a slightly strained voice.

'No more anonymous letters or anything of that sort?'

'No, nothing.'

'That's fine. Well, I mustn't keep you from that pile of briefs, but now that our paths have recrossed, we must meet again soon. One evening next week maybe.'

'That'd be fun, Tony.'

Lelaker rang off as it was on the point of Adam's tongue to propose an earlier meeting. A meeting at which he would seek Tony's advice, for he would certainly know how Adam should handle the present situation. Moreover, it would have been a relief to have shared with someone the memory of his alarming experience. But the moment had passed and Lelaker had rung off. And on second thoughts perhaps it was better not to tell him, since he would probably have embarked with huge zest on some outrageous piece of cloak and dagger nonsense.

At lunch-time, Adam went across to Hall in an altogether less oppressed frame of mind. Indeed he was able to concentrate on his table companion's conversation sufficiently to be bored by an endless discourse on the development of canon law in the fourteenth century.

It had required only a short time at the Bar to convince Adam that, though bores were to be found in all walks of life, there was something about the law that produced the most crashing brand of all. A legal training seemed to nourish better than anything else all the more deplorable facets of the potential bore.

Charles Imrey was back in chambers when Adam returned and gave him a wry smile as he came into the room.

'It seems you made quite an impression on my instructing solicitor yesterday.'

'Creedy, do you mean?'

'Yes, I shouldn't be surprised if he didn't send you some work.'

'I thought you told me that William wasn't very keen on him.'

'I did, but it's better than nothing, isn't it?' He looked meaningly at Adam's virtually bare table. 'Admittedly most of his clients are pretty undesirable specimens, and by the time old Creedy's milked them, they're insolvent as well, but after all someone has to stand up in court and say what cruelly misjudged creatures they are.'

'As you did for Young, for instance.'

'The jury thought so too', Imrey said lightly.

'You haven't heard anything further about the case, I suppose?'

'What should I have heard?' Imrey's tone was suddenly sharp. 'The case is over and finished with as far as I'm concerned – as far as you're concerned too for that matter.'

Adam said nothing but trusted that his colleague was being more prophetic than he realized.

The remainder of the afternoon passed uneventfully and at seven o'clock Adam went round to Sara's to have supper.

He ran up the three flights of stairs to the flat where she lived and pressed the bell. Sara opened the door almost immediately and they kissed. Then standing back and giving her an appraising stare, he said in a faintly accusing tone, 'You've got a new hair-do.'

'Yes, do you like it?'

'It makes you look somehow different.'

Sara sighed. 'So would a poke bonnet.'

Fond though she was of Adam, she did not propose

surrendering her tastes entirely to his, particularly since there was still much of the conservative schoolboy in him which recoiled with horror from the ridiculous in feminine appearance. And as everyone knew, you couldn't be fashionable without often looking mildly ridiculous.

'Come on in and have a drink. One of the firm's clients gave me a bottle of vodka today. He's manager of a wine shop.'

'I've not even had a glass of milk out of any of mine.'

Adam followed her into the living-room of the flat which she shared with two other girls. It was a room in which feminine skill and artifice had achieved wonders with a haphazard assortment of second-hand furniture and fittings.

'How are Mary and Juliet?' he asked, inquiring after her companions.

'They're all right, except that Juliet's starting a cold and was a bit peeved at having to go out tonight.'

The three girls had a strictly adhered-to arrangement whereby each had the flat to herself for one evening a week to entertain friend or friends. On the other four nights only guests acceptable to all were allowed, and although Adam came within this category, he also invariably had supper in the flat alone with Sara on her evening.

'What do you want with your vodka?' he asked, sniffing at the top of the bottle.

'Tonic, I suppose, we haven't got anything else. You?'

'Neat. Like the Kremlin boys.'

Armed with drinks, they went into the kitchen where Adam propped himself against the sink and watched Sara prepare their meal.

'Smells good. What is it, a stew?' he asked hungrily, as she opened the oven door.

'You could call it stew if you wished to be completely peasant, but in fact it's a *casserole de boeuf bordelaise.*' She closed the oven door and handed him a dirty fork to wash. 'Tell me about the case yesterday.'

'I'll get another drink first, if I may.'

'Don't go and pass out before the meal.'

'Of course I shan't. This stuff's not all that strong. The Russians knock it back like pink gargle, and theirs is much fiercer.'

Under the influence of his second drink, Adam began to relate to Sara not only what had happened in court but also his subsequent adventures. The vodka had given him a pleasant sense of euphoria and this, coupled with her rapt attention, caused him to warm to his theme and give the whole story the air of one of James Bond's lesser exploits.

'But what are you going to do now?' she asked anxiously when he had finished.

'Nothing', he replied blandly.

'But you must do something.'

'What?'

There was a few seconds silence before she said in a thoughtful tone, 'Do you think we should go back there after supper?'

'To Warren Place, do you mean?'

Sarah nodded.

'No, I do not. Anyway what should we do when we got there?'

'Find out about Carole Young and the note.'

'You're as bad as Tony. He'd have wanted to rush in and behave like a mad boy scout.' He made a purposeful move away from the sink. 'Come on, let's have that *casserole de boeuf bordelaise*. I'm hungry.'

It was with an abstracted air, however, that Sara dished up, and Adam feared the worst. It was flattering in a way that she took the matter so seriously and he still did not regret having unburdened himself of his secret. Nevertheless he hoped she was not going to be too troublesome, for he had no intention of taking any further independent action, and the only alternative was to tell the police. And there were at least a hundred sound reasons why that course was out of the question.

'But who on earth would have used your name on the note, and why?' she asked when they'd carried the food into the other room.

Adam sighed wearily. 'I haven't the glimmer of an idea.'

'Are you sure you didn't see anyone at court behaving at all suspiciously?'

'Quite . . . well, actually, now you mention it, there was a fellow who caught my attention once or twice. But he can't have had anything to do with it.'

'What was he doing?'

'I first noticed him in court, he appeared to be following the case with particular interest. And then in the luncheon adjournment, I saw him in earnest conversation with Creedy, that's Young's solicitor.'

'Yes?' Sara's eyes were shining eagerly.

'And then he bumped into me when Mrs. Young came up to speak to me in the corridor after the case was over.'

61

'That's significant', she said with scarcely suppressed excitement. 'This man, did he look a sinister type?'

'As a matter of fact he looked rather nice.'

'What age?'

'Early thirties, and tall. I definitely remember his being tall.'

'Who do you think he might have been?'

'No idea. I don't know if Charles might know.'

'You must ask him.'

'Look, my sweet, don't get so enthusiastic. If ever there was a time for mouselike discretion, it's now; unless you want to get me disbarred.'

'I still think we ought to do something.' Her tone became dreamy. 'Perhaps if I were to go up there on my own . . .'

Adam looked up from his plate in startled dismay. 'You mustn't do any such thing.' He shivered at the very prospect. Now that the effect of the vodka was wearing off his instinct was once more to bury the whole episode as deep down in his subconscious as it would go.

When the meal was over and they had cleared away the dishes, he put on some records and lay agreeably on the floor with his head resting in Sara's lap and her hands running gently over his face.

'You're falling asleep', she said suddenly, bending down and giving him a light kiss.

Adam smothered a yawn.

'What's the time?'

'Ten to eleven.'

'I suppose the girls'll be back any minute.'

'Probably.'

'I'd better go. I hardly slept at all last night.'

62

Sara watched him with a worried expression as he got up and stretched luxuriously.

She accompanied him downstairs to the street door and they kissed good night.

Ten minutes after arriving home, Adam was in bed and asleep.

CHAPTER SIX

HE AWOKE the next morning refreshed and with the events of thirty-six hours before seeming to belong to another era. He was never one, however, to spring from his bed with a joyful greet-the-new-day expression on his face and, indeed, found getting up in the morning one of the more difficult tasks. But as he padded about his room wearing one sock and looking for the other, he felt relatively cheerful, and from what he could see of the weather from his window, it promised to be a really hot day. Sunlight already poured into the tiny area (Miss Brown referred to it always as the garden) on to which his bedroom faced.

As usual he was the last down to breakfast. The dining-room, which was deserted, smelt strongly of finnan-haddock and burnt toast. Adam sat down and pushed away a pile of dirty cups and plates in his vicinity.

A minute or two later, Florence, the maid, hobbled in carrying a coffee-pot in one hand and a boiled egg in the other.

'Oh, you going to sit that end, Mr. Cape?'

'I've already cleared a space here, Floss. How are you this morning?'

'My corns ain't half giving me gyp. Must be the weather.'

'But it's a glorious day.'

'It'll rain', Florence observed flatly, plonking her load down in front of him.

'I thought it was haddock this morning.'

'It was, but it's finished. Mr. Asmani had the last. I've done you an egg.'

'How long have you given it?' He asked suspiciously, tapping it with a spoon. 'Sounds as hard as a rubber ball.'

'Done just to your liking, Mr. Cape', she replied equably as she overpoured the coffee into his saucer and splashed the piece of toast he was about to take.

'God help your husband, Floss, if ever you get one', Adam said, giving her a friendly pat on the behind. She gave him a fearful leer and sidled back to her kitchen. Though all of sixty she frequently dropped dark hints about an improbable boy-friend who was waiting only for the right moment (never defined) to take her up the aisle.

Happily, Adam's hunger was sufficient to allow him to overlook the shortcomings of his breakfast. As he poured himself out a second cup of coffee, he reached over for a paper which had been thrown down on a chair.

His eye skimmed over the front page news, alighting only with interest on a paragraph about the domestic troubles of a well-known actor. He was about to turn to the sports page when a two-line item in the stop-press hit him like a short-swung cosh.

'Woman's body found in North London Canal.'

Feverishly he tore through the rest of the paper, though realizing he wouldn't find anything further. If the item had only just made the stop-press, there'd hardly be any other reference to it.

Jumping from his chair, he searched the room for another paper. A later edition might well have further particulars. But there wasn't one. Then he remembered that Florence usually sneaked one out of the room to read over her own breakfast.

'Let me see that paper a moment, Floss', he said urgently as he burst into the kitchen.

Meekly surrendering the newspaper, Florence gazed at him in astonishment.

'You had a shock or something, Mr. Cape?'

But Adam ignored her in his desperate attention to the paper he had seized out of her hands.

There was nothing in it, however, and with a muttered word of thanks he returned to the dining-room and anxiously studied the original item again.

'Woman's body found in North London Canal.'

Why had he jumped to conclusions? After all, if one believed all one read, dozens of bodies were fished out of London's rivers and canals every week, and a large proportion of them must presumably be women. And even if, against all odds, this *was* Carole Young's body, there was no suggestion that there had been anything other than an accident. Thus did his defence mechanism hasten to the rescue. But there was no denying the fact it had shaken him. He'd see if he could buy a paper with more news on his way to chambers.

Armed with no less than six, he fought his way into a Circle Line train to find it would have been impossible to read a postage stamp, let alone unfold a newspaper. He hurried out of the Temple Station and to the same coffee-bar in which he and Tony Lelaker had happened to meet that mistily distant afternoon ten days before.

Unaware and unminding that he was the centre of mild interest as he intently scanned one newspaper after another, he completed his search without having gleaned anything further. All he could now do was wait for the midday editions of the evening papers.

He found it more difficult than ever to concentrate his mind that morning on the fodder of a legal career, and in particular on the niceties of the Hire Purchase Regulations.

About noon, Charles Imrey came back from court and flinging down a pile of documents on his table said crisply, 'I see they've fished your chief witness out of a canal.'

'Where did you see that?' Adam asked, trying to sound no more interested than the news would warrant.

'It's all over the front page of the midday papers.'

'Have you got one there?'

'Gave it to William.'

'Oh.'

'Go and ask him for it if you're all that interested.'

'Of course I'm interested.' Adam laughed nervously. 'Have any of your witnesses ever drowned themselves immediately after a case?'

'Don't be facetious, Adam! And anyway this woman didn't drown herself.'

Adam caught his breath. 'What happened then?'

'She was strangled.'

'Oh, no.'

It was a cry of anguish and Imrey looked at him curiously.

'For heaven's sake, don't get morbid about it.'

'Does the paper say who did it?'

'No; only that the police are searching for her husband.'

'Do you think he did it?'

'My dear Adam, I'm not a detective. But he's a pretty obvious suspect.'

'And he's disappeared?'

'Apparently.'

Adam left chambers in a daze and buying copies of all the midday papers and some sandwiches, went and sat in the shade of a tree on the embankment.

The papers added little further to his knowledge, but now that he knew that the dead woman was indeed Carole Young and that she had been murdered, it made his position in one sense somewhat easier. There was now less reason than ever for his going to the police. They were already searching for her husband and once he was found, the case would be as good as over. He'd had the clearest possible motive for killing his wife and had done so within hours of being acquitted of the charge of assaulting her.

Adam felt a sudden angry resentment against Frankie Young. Not only had he worsted Adam in court, but he had then had the effrontery to use his name to lure an unsuspecting wife to her death.

In the act of biting into a sandwich, Adam froze. The note! Where was the note! Surely the police must find it when they searched her pockets or handbag.

He groaned aloud. There was, of course, the faint hope that she had put it in her handbag and that this had not been recovered. As he sat suddenly chilled with fright on a superb summer's day, Carole Young's anxious face floated before his mind's eye. 'May I speak to you, sir . . . I must talk to someone.' Her pathetic plea echoed in his ears. And what had been his response? To brush her aside. And now she was dead, murdered, and he, Adam, hiding in her flat like a sneak-thief must have been almost the last person to have seen her. Except that he hadn't actually seen her, though he could have put out a hand and touched her.

It was in a grim mood that he went back to chambers.

'Miss Sloman phoned twice while you were out', William said as Adam tried to slip past his door unseen. 'She asked if you would call her at her office when you came back.'

'Thanks.'

'It's sad about Mrs. Young's death,' William went on, 'but you mustn't get too personally involved in your cases, Mr. Cape. It's not a wise thing to do in court, but it's much worse out of court.'

Adam conjured up a wan smile and passed on to his room to phone Sara before Charles Imrey returned.

'What are you going to do now?' she asked in an urgent whisper, as soon as she heard his voice.

'I must think a while. I'd sooner not talk about it on the phone.' Adam had no reason to suspect William of listening in to phone calls on the chambers exchange but he was taking no chances. Moreover, he did wish to think.

'All right, darling, give me a ring at the flat about six.' There was a pause. 'Adam?'

'Yes?'

'I love you.' Without waiting for a reply she rang off, leaving him to ponder the ill-starred moment of her declaration. He knew he should feel grateful for her loyalty and affection. Instead, he regarded them as adding to his troubles.

At the moment all he wanted was to be left alone to sort

out his thoughts. He didn't want Sara or Tony or anyone else trying to help him with advice and suggestions. Later he might be glad to receive them, but not now.

When he left chambers after an afternoon of desperate heart-searching, he bought yet another batch of papers and retired again to the coffee-bar to read them. A perusal of the front page of the first, however, sufficed to clear his mind, for there immediately beneath a headline appeared the following ominous paragraph :

'The police are anxious to trace a man who was seen in Warren Place about ten o'clock the evening before last. A passer-by directed the man to the home of the deceased and he was seen to cross the road and enter it. He is described as being between twenty and thirty years old, about 5 ft. 6 ins. tall, slim build, and with a sallow complexion.

It is thought that this man may be able to assist the police in their investigation.

Meanwhile an intensive search continues for the dead woman's husband, who has not been seen since his acquittal at the Old Bailey. . . .'

CHAPTER SEVEN

IT WAS from the evening paper that Adam learnt too that Detective-Superintendent Manton of the Divisional C.I.D. was in charge of the investigation. He knew him by name but no more. A quarter of an hour later, however, he was speaking to him on the telephone.

'My name is Adam Cape and I think I may have some information about the Young case which might interest you.'

'Mr. Cape, did you say?'

'Yes, I'm a barrister.'

'Of course, sir, I thought I knew your name, you prosecuted Young.'

'Yes. I was wondering if I could come and have a talk to you, Superintendent.'

'I don't want to put you to that trouble, sir, I'll come and see you. Perhaps you can give me an idea what it's about.'

'It'll be no trouble and I'd prefer to come to you.' To himself Adam's voice sounded as though it was coming from some disembodied agency.

Manton noted a suppressed urgency in this caller's tone and was curious. 'O.K., Mr. Cape, when would you like to come?'

'Now?'

'Fine.'

Half an hour later, Adam was sitting in Manton's office at the headquarters of — Division in North London.

'Well, now, sir, what's it all about?' Manton asked quietly, fixing Adam with a pair of keen blue eyes.

Though during the past half-hour he had rehearsed what he was going to say, till he was satisfied he had achieved exactly the right nuance of expression, it now came out in one breathless rush. 'I'm the man who was seen going into the Youngs' house.'

Manton's astonishment was manifest. 'You, sir?'

Without further encouragement, Adam plunged into his story and omitting no detail told Manton everything.

There was a long silence when he had finished, during which Manton's eyes never left his face. But Adam was hardly aware of the intense scrutiny to which he was being subjected, for the nervous effort of talking had left him physically limp and mentally drained.

'If I may say so, Mr. Cape, you seem to have behaved in a very unorthodox manner for a member of the Bar.'

With an effort, Adam focused his attention.

'Eh?'

'I said that your behaviour seems to have been most unusual for a member of your profession.'

'I suppose so.'

'When we put out that description, we were looking for a murderer.'

Adam's heart skipped a beat.

'But surely that's the husband?'

'Well, the description isn't far off that of Young. He's about your height and build. His hair's straight, of course, and I wouldn't have described you as sallow. Your complexion is more a healthy tan, I'd say.'

'It was dark and the street lighting wasn't exactly flattering.'

There was another pause, then Manton went on, 'I wonder, sir, if you'd mind being confronted by the old boy who says he saw the man go into the house?'

'Do you mean an identification parade?'

'Good heavens, no! I'd just like him to have a look at you here in my office and see whether he recognizes you.'

Adam realized that this was a first polite manoeuvre to check his story. If the old boy failed to recognize him, Manton would probably send him home and offer him soothing advice to visit his doctor in the morning.

But when not long after the old man was brought into Manton's office and asked in an almost indifferent tone, 'Ever seen that gentleman before?' he screwed up his eyes and, glaring at Adam, said, 'Yes, that looks like him.'

'Now are you satisfied?' Adam asked when the old man had gone out again. But Manton ignored the question.

'This note you saw on the table, are you quite sure it bore your name?'

'Of course I am. I probably shouldn't have come and seen you but for that. You haven't found it?'

'No.'

'Perhaps when you recover her handbag . . .'

'We have done already, but there was no note in it.'

'Perhaps she threw it away after picking it up off the table.'

Adam's eyes met Manton's and saw a plain mixture of doubt and scepticism.

'You don't believe there was a note, do you?' he said.

Manton gave a slight shrug. 'I can't think why you should take the trouble to come here and tell me all this if it's not true.'

But Adam could detect the note of suspended judgement in his tone.

'Have you any clues as to Young's whereabouts?' he asked.

'At the moment, none. He's vanished completely, though I've no doubt we shall find him sooner or later.'

Adam nodded. He was filled with a sense of hollow anti-climax. He had unburdened himself of his story, but was being neither held in a cell, nor fêted with the Police Commissioner's grateful thanks, both of which possibilities his lively imagination had variously envisaged.

Manton rose from his desk and with a faint smile said, 'Well, thank you for coming, Mr. Cape. I shall have to report your visit to my superiors, but I suggest meanwhile that you don't tell anyone about it yourself. Indeed I would ask you *not* to do so. I'll get in touch with you, probably tomorrow, when we may have made some progress.' His smile flickered. 'Some *more* progress.'

Adam felt dispirited and uncertain and was aware that Manton was watching him with curious interest.

'It probably sounds silly to you, Superintendent, but this is as close as I've ever been to sudden death, and I can't help feeling partially responsible for what's happened.'

'Because you failed to get a conviction against Young?'

'More because I might have been able to help Mrs. Young if I'd listened to what she wanted to tell me.'

'I doubt whether the course of events would have been different, if that's any salve to your conscience.'

'They must have been different if Young had still been in prison.'

'True.'

Adam moved towards the door of the oppressively stuffy office.

'Whereabouts was Mrs. Young's body recovered?'

'Twenty yards or so from the bridge mentioned in your note. It had been weighted with stones which had parted from it so that the body came to the surface.'

'Does the pathologist think she was dead before her body was put into the water?'

'He's certain she was.'

Manton opened the door and held it for Adam to go out. It seemed clear that he thought sufficient time had been spent on the interview.

The streets were airless and the evening sky was ominously leaden when Adam emerged. There were few people about and the atmosphere was hot and gritty.

Undecided what to do next, he walked aimlessly down the street. He had gone about two hundred yards when he observed a red sports coupé pull up at the opposite kerb and a tall young man get out and hurry across the pavement into an office building. Even though his glimpse of the man had been short, he at once recognized him as the same tall young man who had attracted his attention at court.

Thoroughly intrigued, and with his weariness forgotten, he crossed the road and approached the building which the man had entered. A list of the tenants just inside the entrance showed that on the first floor was 'Cecil Creedy, Solicitor and Commissioner for Oaths'.

Adam strolled on and for the next ten minutes showed an inordinate interest in a shop window which was full of cheap furniture of a hideous design. But no one came out of the solicitor's building during this time and after making a quick note of the car's registration number, he decided to go home. On the morrow he would call someone he knew who worked in the car licensing department of the L.C.C. to find out the name of the car's owner. It seemed a reasonable presumption that it belonged to the tall young man.

Moreover, he was glad now that he had not mentioned the latter's existence to Manton, though at the time his failure to do so had been simply to avoid sounding melodramatic.

It was in a mood of unwarranted but mild elation that he reached Kensington.

He had hardly let himself into the house before Sara came dashing into the hall.

'Where've you been all this time, Adam? You never phoned me as you said you would. I've been terribly worried.'

'I'm very sorry, but there's no need for you to have been', he replied, a trifle nettled by her admonitory tone. 'What are you doing here anyway?'

'Oh, Adam!'

'Now what?'

'Didn't it occur to you that I should be worried when you didn't call, particularly after I'd read the evening papers and seen about the man they wanted to trace?'

'Ssh!' he hissed, glancing anxiously down the passage.

Sara looked contrite. 'It's all right, I haven't told a soul.'

'And you mustn't either.'

'Tell me what you've been doing. Have you been to the police?'

'Come on, we'll go out and find a quiet corner to talk. Does Miss Brown know you're here?'

'She's out. Florence let me in.'

Adam gave a shout in the direction of the kitchen. 'Floss, I'm back and just going out again. Miss Sloman and I want to drink your health, we're going to the Blue Boar.'

They walked to the public house and found an unoccupied corner in the saloon bar. Adam brought over a pint of bitter and a lemon shandy, lit a cigarette and then gave Sara an account of his movements.

'I suppose you had to tell the police really', she said when he had finished. 'You don't think they suspect you of anything, do you?'

'What, for instance?'

'I don't know.'

'Well, thank you for something! As a matter of fact, the Superintendent was extremely guarded, though I can't say I entirely blame him. Members of the Bar are usually more circumspect than I've been. As it is, if this takes any further nasty turns, I could easily find myself on the mat in front of the Benchers.' He paused to ponder a moment, then gave Sara a wry grin. 'However, in for a penny, in for a pound.'

'Ah, there you both are', a voice exclaimed, as Adam turned to see Tony Lelaker advancing towards them, followed by the ineffable Debbie. 'The maid at your place said we'd find you here.'

'Hi', Debbie said, sitting down next to Adam.

Lelaker made his way to the bar and a few minutes later

returned with some drinks. Debbie had asked for stout, rather to Adam's surprise.

'Now then, Adam, let's hear all', Tony said eagerly, as he drew up a chair and sat down with a smile which embraced them all.

'All of what?'

'All of what's been happening, of course. You're not going to tell me that the Yard haven't taken you into their confidence.'

This approach was much too enthusiastic for Adam's liking and he felt himself begin to sprout prickles. 'The case is being handled by the Division', he said coolly. 'Scotland Yard are not directly concerned with it.'

'Come off the technicalities, Adam, you know what I mean. Have the police been in touch with you yet, and if so what have you told them?' Lelaker grinned good-naturedly. 'Don't forget that I'm your bodyguard.'

'There's nothing much *I* can help the police about', Adam said, giving Sara a quick meaningful glance.

'But surely they're interested in the fact that you received those threatening letters before the trial and then immediately it's all over the chief witness is found murdered.'

'If they are, they haven't taken me into their confidence.'

'Who do they think murdered Carole Young?'

'I imagine they suspect her husband.'

'What about the chap they want to interview who was seen going into the Youngs' house?'

Adam frowned into his beer. Why couldn't Tony shut up? 'That could have been the husband too. The description fits him, more or less.'

Debbie, who had paid no attention to the conversation,

now drained her glass and quietly drew Tony Lelaker's attention to it. When he had gone to fetch her another, she looked morosely at Sara and said, 'Tony's trouble is that he has too much energy for one. He can't bear to think he may be missing someone else's fun.'

Adam smiled. He liked the astringent streak behind the dumb-blonde façade. 'But I'm not having fun', he said.

'It's fun to him.'

Lelaker returned with the drinks and sat down again. 'What have you been telling Sara and Adam about me?' he asked pleasantly, after a quick glance at their faces.

'Just that you always want to take more out of life than other people have energy to put into it', Debbie observed, with a yawn.

The conversation became desultory, and it was not until they got up to leave that Lelaker returned to the original topic.

'Why don't we do a bit of sleuthing on our own, Adam? Try and find out who sent you those letters and that sort of thing. We might be able to help the police.'

'We'd be much more likely to get a severe rap over the knuckles. That mightn't matter to you, but it would put finis to my career.'

Lelaker shook his head mournfully. 'Trouble is, Adam, that though you pretend not to be starry-eyed about your profession, you're about as conventionally-minded as a Victorian judge.' He caught the smile that flickered across Adam's face. 'What's so funny about that?'

'Nothing.'

'Oh, well, some people have all the excitement and fun, and then don't know how to make the most of it.'

It was after they had parted and Adam was walking home with Sara that she said, 'I should think Tony would be a jolly good person to have beside you in a tight corner.'

'I'd prefer Debbie.'

'I'm glad to see you looking better this morning, Mr. Cape', William said when Adam arrived at chambers the next morning.

'Any of those for me?' Adam asked, nodding at a load of pink-taped briefs on the clerk's table.

'I fear not, but your practice is coming along nicely, sir. I was looking at your fee book only yesterday evening . . .'

'That must have made light reading.'

'It shows slow but sure progress.'

'Too slow. At the present rate, I'll be fifty before I'm earning a thousand a year.'

William sighed. The theme was familiar to him and accounted for the number of likeable and promising young barristers who left the Bar each year to seek their bread and butter elsewhere; as civil servants or as legal advisers to big companies.

'What's more,' Adam went on, breaking in on the clerk's wistful contemplation of an under-nourished junior profession, 'when one has earned a few guineas, it apparently needs every device of modern torture to get the money out of the solicitors.'

William shook his head reprovingly, but without great conviction. It was all too true that there were many solicitors who were disgracefully dilatory in paying counsel's fees.

'Hello, Adam, you bellyaching to William about fees?' Robert Canfield asked, coming into the clerk's room.

'Yes.'

'Quite right too. I'm owed over five hundred pounds for cases which were completed the year before last and in which, moreover, I happen to know the lay client settled up immediately.'

'I'll get in touch with the solicitors again today', William said hastily, and the small indignation meeting broke up.

Adam went to his room and at once put through a call to County Hall.

'May I speak to Miss Hayley, please', he chanted dully as he was put through to a succession of wrong extensions.

Eventually, however, he recognized the voice that answered him.

'Isobel, this is Adam Cape. Remember me? – haven't seen you for ages. Look, Isobel, I wonder if you could possibly help me by telling me off the record who's the registered owner of 6437 CLO?'

'That shouldn't be too difficult, Adam. I'll call you back within ten minutes.'

While he waited, Adam wondered what use he was going to make of the information when he had it. Of course it would depend to a certain extent on what it was.

His extension phone rang and he lifted the receiver with a tingle of excitement.

'I've got the information you want, Adam', Isobel announced in her clear business-like tone. 'The owner is a Roger Winslow whose address is shown as 18, Wells Road, Ealing, W.5.'

'Thanks awfully, Isobel.'

'A pleasure. See you one day, maybe?'

He rang off and noticed that Charles Imrey had come into the room and was standing watching him.

'What would Sara say if she knew you were phoning strange women called Isobel?' he asked roguishly.

Adam smiled agreeably. He was used to what Charles Imrey was pleased to call good-natured chaff and which covered everything from the offensive to facetious comment on Adam's behaviour, appearance and general existence.

'Forgetting Isobel if you can,' he said, 'did you notice a tall young man in court during the Young trial?'

'No. The court may have been stiff with tall young men for all I know.'

'This particular one seemed to know your instructing solicitor. I saw them talking together at one stage.'

Charles Imrey shrugged his shoulders. 'Anyway what was so interesting about him?'

'I just wondered whether you'd noticed him and, if so, whether you knew who he was.'

Imrey's eyes narrowed as he fixed Adam with a cross-examination stare. 'What on earth's come over you since that case? You seem to have developed a fixation about it and about everyone who was in court at the time.'

Adam looked enigmatic and Imrey sounded crosser when he went on. 'Have you been up to something fishy? You've really behaved most strangely.'

'It's your lively imagination, Charles.'

'I hope it is. We don't want chambers dragged into anything unethical.'

'I'll try and remember that', Adam said through clenched

82

teeth and left the room. 'I'm going for a coffee', he called out to William as he passed his door.

Middle Temple Lane greeted him with sunshine and for a few seconds he paused in the doorway and gazed at the dark-suited servants of the law who passed to and fro and disappeared down narrow alleyways, exchanging languid greetings or looking gravely pensive.

A youth carrying a fat envelope paused beside Adam and studied the panel of names just inside the doorway.

'Mr. Canfield's chambers?' he asked.

'Down the passage, last door on the right.'

'Thanks.'

Adam continued to study the eight names on the board, the last of which was 'Mr. Adam Cape'.

Then with a resigned shrug of his shoulders, he went in search of coffee.

When he left chambers that evening he walked to the Temple Station and caught an Ealing train.

Maybe he *was* doing the very thing which Sara and Tony Lelaker had urged as a joint enterprise, but he was doing it in his own way and for the moment he preferred it should be so.

Wells Road was not far from the Common and contained a number of new houses of stockbroker Tudor design, each with about a third of an acre of carefully tended garden.

Number 18 was one of these, slightly smaller than its neighbours, but their equal in every other respect.

A rather pleasant-looking woman with neatly-waved grey hair was busily engaged with a trowel and a tray of small plants. She didn't look up as Adam passed by on the opposite pavement.

The garage doors were open and he could see the red sports coupé parked inside.

The road, which was entirely residential, was almost deserted and Adam realized that he would soon draw attention to himself if he hung about. Indeed, he trusted there would not be any burglaries in the district that night or he might easily find his description in the newspapers once more. Luckily, however, the road was lined with bushy chestnut trees which provided shade and a fair amount of cover to his movements.

He was about to stroll on when the front door of the house opened and the tall young man came out. He was dressed in flannels and a blazer and was wearing a striped club tie, and looked nothing so much as a very ordinary and amiable young man. He walked across to where the woman was gardening and they conversed for a minute or two. Then with a flip of his hand he strolled towards the garage.

'What time will you be in, Roger?' the woman called out.

'Probably after you've gone to bed, Mother.'

He backed the car out into the road and with a final friendly wave to the woman shot down the road in a burst of second-gear speed.

Adam walked on in the opposite direction with a purposeful expression, which he assumed for the benefit of any curious passer-by.

It seemed a pity to leave the area without trying to find out a little more about the occupants of 18, Wells Road, and it was with this thought in mind that he entered a near-by public house. It was a few minutes after seven and the saloon bar was deserted apart from a couple of men and a girl sitting over at a corner table.

'Not much doing tonight', he observed pleasantly to the publican who drew him a pint of draught bitter.

'Bit early yet. This is 'twixt and between time. Those who drop in for a pint on their way home have been and gone, and our evening regulars haven't arrived yet.'

Adam leaned against the bar in relaxed comfort. 'Do you get much custom from the people who live around here? I mean, I happened to come along – Wells Road is it? – just now and I wouldn't have thought the people who lived in those sort of houses frequented pubs very much.'

'You're quite wrong about that, sir. Public houses don't have any class barrier. You from abroad by the way?'

Slightly taken aback, Adam admitted that he was but didn't add that he had lived in England for the past sixteen years. 'I thought you must be or you'd have known that everyone from a duke to a dustman is at home in a pub. Now take Wells Road, which you mentioned just now, I reckon that at least eighty per cent of the people who live in those houses come in here regularly, some more than others, mark you.'

'There are some nice-looking houses in that road', Adam said.

'Very nice indeed.'

'With lovely gardens, too. I particularly liked the one at number 20.'

The publican's brow furrowed with the effort of recollection.

'You must be thinking of number 18. Number 20's a bit overgrown. The old lady there died recently and the new owner hasn't moved in yet. But Mrs. Winslow at number 18, she really has got green fingers.'

85

'It must have been her I saw. Has she got a red car?'

'That's Mr. Roger's car. He's her son.'

'Lucky chap.'

'He's in the trade, he should know how to get the best.'

There was a pause while Adam took a gulp of beer and wondered whether he could innocently steer the conversation any further.

'Does he specialize in Jags?'

'No, he's a general dealer, has a place near the White City. Does pretty well too.'

'I bought a car from a dealer near there a year or so ago', Adam lied. 'What's the name of his firm, it might be the same place.'

'Winslow Motors.'

Adam nodded and finished his beer. 'Happen to hear what the West Indies final score was?'

'A hundred and sixty-four for three. Looks like being a draw. That's the trouble with first-class cricket these days, too many drawn matches.'

For the next five minutes they discussed cricket, a subject about which, as it turned out, each held vigorous views.

When Adam came to leave, he hoped that all recollection of his discreetly pointed interest in the Winslow family had been effaced from the publican's mind.

It was Friday evening. Sara had gone to spend the week-end in the country with the family of one of her flat companions, and Adam had no particular plans.

As he made his way back to Kensington, however, he had a shrewd idea how he was going to spend at least part of the time.

CHAPTER EIGHT

MATHER BROTHERS LTD., bookbinders and printers, had premises in Packhorse Road, N.10. This much, Adam remembered from his brief in the Young case. From the same source he also knew that Frankie Young had been one of their storemen at the time of the offence which had taken him into the dock of the Old Bailey.

On the next morning, which was muggy and overcast, Adam made his way through the amorphous inner suburbs and after what seemed an endless journey was put down on a street corner a hundred yards from Messrs. Mathers' premises.

Packhorse Road was long and a typical product of the haphazard growth of the first thirty years of the century, though Adam reckoned that the building owned by Mather Brothers Ltd. must be one of the oldest in the street and date back before then. This was confirmed by the plaque beside the main entrance which said, 'Established 1885'.

Beside this, pinned to the main door was a notice which read, 'Closed from Friday, 2nd August to Monday, 19th August for staff holidays.'

A man came out while Adam was still reading it.

'Can I help you? We close at one o'clock today, you know.' As an afterthought, he added, 'You're not police, are

you?' Adam shook his head in slight alarm at the suddenness of the question. 'I only asked because we've had them
around a fair amount the last day or so.'

'Oh.'

'Yes, that fellow Young whom they're looking for. You
know, the bloke whose wife was found murdered a couple of
days ago. He used to work here.'

'Oh, yes, I've read about the case. He's not employed
here any more then?'

'He hasn't worked here since he was arrested a month
ago, and after this latest I shouldn't think they'd be very
keen to have him back at all, even if it were possible.'

'What sort of chap was he?'

'Pretty average sort of bloke.'

'Wonder what's happened to him. Mysterious the way
he disappeared after the trial and hasn't been seen since.'

'Someone's hiding him, otherwise they'd have found him
by now.'

'You could be right, I suppose. On the other hand it's
possible he's on the run.'

The man shook his head vigorously. 'Young wouldn't
have the *nous*. You mark my words, someone's hiding him.'

'But who and why?'

'Search me, I'm not a copper. And anyway, what's your
interest?'

Adam felt himself blushing under the man's now suddenly
hostile stare.

'Someone I know was connected with the case, that's all.'

'Oh! Well, I don't know why I'm standing on the step
talking to you when I've got work to do.'

The man – Adam guessed he was probably a foreman –

returned inside and Adam resumed his study of the exterior of the premises. So this was the building which Frankie Young had left one evening a month before to go home and have a violent quarrel with his wife, in the course of which he had either stabbed her or, according to him, she had stabbed herself.

With these thoughts passing through his mind, he walked on past the new bank which had gone up next door, past the adjoining supermarket and then across to the tobacconist on the opposite side, which he entered.

The shop had a hot, musty smell of tobacco and newspapers and the old woman in a pinafore behind the counter left her only other customer to serve him. As Adam pocketed the cigarettes and she counted out his change, he glanced at the man waiting at his side. He was a thick-set and formidable-looking man who returned Adam's glance with an unfriendly glower.

Adam's own expression reflected cool dislike.

Outside the shop, he paused and gazed across at Mather Brothers' low, straggling premises before walking to the bus-stop. A sixpenny ride brought him to the neighbourhood of Warren Place. But this time it was the canal, and not the Youngs' house, which drew him.

'Meet me under the canal bridge at the end of Mulhouse Street', the murderer had written.

Mulhouse Street was a short, terraced cul-de-sac. At its end, a narrow footpath ran between two high fences to lead to a footbridge over the canal. At the side of the ramp of the bridge, rough steps led down to the towpath. The whole scene was uninviting in the extreme and the canal water looked as though greasy dishes were constantly washed in it.

Adam slithered down the steps and turned under the arch of the bridge. The path here was no more than three feet wide and one could only stand upright on the absolute edge.

So this was the scene of murder, now doubtless captured by the cold lens of the police photographer.

Adam shivered. He felt suddenly chilled by the sinister atmosphere which persisted there, and stepped quickly out into the open.

It was still a warm Saturday in July, but standing there beneath the bridge he had felt suddenly encompassed by the hidden forces of unknown evil.

CHAPTER NINE

Aᴏᴛᴇʀ having a snack lunch Adam decided to go for a
swim, with the further possibility of going to a cinema
later in the afternoon.

He spent a couple of hours at the pool, though it was more
crowded than he liked. He had nimbly hauled his dripping
body out of the water for the last time and was sitting on the
edge in a mood of relaxed contentment when George came
up.

'Hello, Mr. Cape, sir, haven't had time to talk to you this
afternoon. Had a good swim?'

'Fine, thanks.'

The grizzled attendant gazed at a couple of porpoise-sized
males thrashing about at the far side.

'Horrible sights!' he said, scornfully squatting on his
haunches beside Adam and casting an approving look at his
firm, brown body. 'Been seeing your name in the papers
recently.'

Adam looked up quickly. 'That case I did at the Old
Bailey you mean?'

The other nodded. 'Bad luck on his wife getting
murdered like that.' This seemed to be carrying British
understatement a little far. 'Suppose there's no doubt it was
her husband what strangled her?'

'Looks that way.'

There was a sudden splash, followed by a resentful bellow and George hurried off to where a fully-clothed, tubby boy was clambering out of the pool, and yelling at two other boys who were doubled up with laughter on the edge. Adam seized the diversion to go and get dressed.

It was four o'clock when he emerged, and he decided to go to a cinema before returning to his lodgings.

He reached home about half past seven to learn that Charles Imrey had been calling him almost hourly since eleven o'clock that morning and wished to speak to him most urgently.

Adam wondered what on earth he could want, and felt certain only that whatever it was was likely to reveal an ulterior motive.

It was while he was pondering whether to call back before or after his supper that Imrey phoned again.

'I've been trying to get you all day, Adam. I did leave a message asking that you should phone me as soon as you came in.'

'I have only just come in.'

'Look Adam, I'm in a fix on Monday morning and I'd be grateful if you could help me out.'

'How?'

'By doing a bail application before the chambers judge. It won't occupy more than a few minutes, but I have a defended divorce first in the list and I shan't be able to manage the other.'

'O.K. When do I see the papers?'

'I'll drop them in tomorrow morning. I've got to come close by you – lunching with my in-laws in Knightsbridge.'

'Does the solicitor know you won't be turning up?'

'Yes. I told him I'd ask you to stand in for me and he was perfectly satisfied. It's Creedy incidentally. I must go, we've got friends in for drinks.'

Imrey rang off and Adam went thoughtfully up to his room.

Creedy, eh! Well, in the circumstances he relished the prospect of meeting Young's solicitor again. It would provide him with a golden opportunity of finding out more about the mysterious Roger Winslow.

There is a remote enclave of the Royal Courts of Justice, intimate and inviting as a railway waiting-room, known as the Bear Garden and it was thither that Adam directed his footsteps shortly after ten o'clock on the following Monday morning.

At the moment of his arrival it was as deserted as an empty stage, with only an occasional black-coated clerk scurrying out of one door and quickly disappearing through another.

In a particularly dark corner stood a particularly solid-looking door with a list pinned on the wall beside it.

Adam peered at this and saw that 'in re Ananias bail application' was first. Then moving across to where some jaded shafts of light mingled with the atmosphere of brown austerity he unfolded his brief and read it through again. The only document of any substance was an affidavit by Joseph Ananias, setting out in Mr. Creedy's best composition all the reasons why he should be released on bail pending his trial at the September session of the Old Bailey on charges of obtaining money by false pretences.

Adam had never before made a bail application in front

of the judge in chambers, but he gathered from Charles Imrey that all he had to do was read out the affidavit, amplifying it at his discretion, and fix the judge with a pleading look. The only other documents in his possession were a summons taken out by Mr. Creedy requiring the prosecution to show cause why the unfortunate Ananias should not be admitted to bail, and a short affidavit from Mr. Creedy relating to service of the summons upon the Director of Public Prosecutions.

By the time Adam had finished scanning these documents, it was three minutes to half past ten and a milling throng had formed in front of the judge's door. Of Mr. Creedy, however, there was no sign.

There was still no sign of him when the door opened and an official came out and shouted above the din, 'Ananias, bail.'

Adam put his shoulder down and pushed, arriving at the door at the same time as the D.P.P.'s representative and a police officer.

'My instructing solicitor . . .' he began breathlessly to the court official who was waiting to release them through the door into the judge's presence.

'Ready?' the official asked in a harassed tone as almost everyone within view tried to attract his attention at the same time. 'Inside, then.'

As they were catapulted into the judge's presence, Adam became aware that Mr. Creedy had managed to join them from nowhere and was greeting him with sly amusement.

Mr. Justice Corbett, whom Adam knew only as an imposing figure in judicial robes, sat behind a broad table looking very ordinary and faintly wistful without the adornment of wig or scarlet gown. Moreover, Adam, who had always imagined him to be bald was surprised to see that he had a thick thatch of straw-coloured hair.

'Yes, Mr. Cape?' the judge said pleasantly, surveying the line of faces across the table.

'My lord, I appear for the applicant in this matter. He has sworn an affidavit in which . . .'

'Yes, Mr. Cape, I have read the affidavit. Is there anything in addition to it that you would like me to consider?'

'He has a fixed address and is willing to report to the police as required', Mr. Creedy hissed loudly from just behind Adam's left shoulder.

Adam relayed the information to the judge, who nodded politely.

'Anything else, Mr. Cape?'

'He can find sureties up to any amount', hissed Mr. Creedy again.

Adam frowned and passed this on without enthusiasm.

'Tell him, too, that there's no question of interference with any of the prosecution's witnesses', Mr. Creedy continued unabashed.

The judge peered past Adam in the solicitor's direction like a thrush listening to the subterranean vibrations of a worm.

'Yes, thank you, Mr. Cape. Well, what have you got to say about this application, Mr. Sykes?' he asked, turning to the representative of the Director of Public Prosecutions.

'The application is opposed, my lord', Mr. Sykes said emphatically. 'The grounds are that the police have reason to believe the accused may abscond . . .'

'He'll surrender his passport', Mr. Creedy hissed.

95

'. . . and that he would very likely commit further offences of a similar nature. . . .'

'Monstrous suggestion', Mr. Creedy muttered indignantly.

Adam turned and glared at his instructing solicitor, who merely took the opportunity of putting his mouth close to Adam's ear and whispering in a gush of hot breath, 'Don't let them get away with it! The police raise the same old parrot cry every time in these cases. How can he abscond when he has a wife and four children to whom he's devoted? What evidence can there be that he's likely to commit further offences?'

'The reason why the police believe the accused may commit further offences if he is released on bail,' Mr. Sykes went on blandly, as though he had heard Mr. Creedy's whispered commentary, 'is that he has done precisely that on previous occasions.' The judge looked up with interest. 'He has six previous convictions for fraud, my lord, the last of which relates to a sum of £20 which he obtained from a juror at an Assize Court while awaiting his own trial. It appears he required the money to pay for his defence.' Mr. Sykes cast a wry sidelong glance at Mr. Creedy.

'Most enterprising', murmured the judge and looked towards Adam. 'Is there anything further you wish to add?'

Before Adam could speak, Mr. Creedy had prodded him in the ribs.

'Tell him . . .'

But Adam waved him into silence and with the air of one loyally facing defeat in a doubtful cause, said, 'I'm instructed, my lord, that he has a wife and four children whom he supports and is accordingly most unlikely to abscond.'

This time it was the police officer's turn to hiss into the ear of Mr. Sykes, who said smugly, 'I understand, my lord, that the accused has left his wife and that she has taken out a summons for maintenance.'

The judge, with an amused glint in his eye, looked from Mr. Sykes to Adam. 'Yes, Mr. Cape?'

'No, my lord, I don't think that there is anything else I can usefully add.'

Bail was refused, bows were made and a few seconds later they were fighting their way out of the judge's room.

'Come and have a coffee', Mr. Creedy said, as they paused while Adam endorsed his brief. 'Didn't think we had much hope on that one. Fellow has such a shocking record.'

'Is he an old client of yours?'

'He seems to have confidence in me', Mr. Creedy said demurely. 'He always comes to me when he's in trouble, and despite his six convictions, I've got him off more often than otherwise.'

On leaving the Law Courts, Mr. Creedy led the way to a small dingy café which smelt of cigarette ends.

'Coffee?' he asked when a waitress slipped up to their table.

'Please.'

'Never see any point in paying sevenpence or eightpence for a cup of coffee when you get one here for sixpence.'

The coffee which came was brown and tasted of acorns, but Adam didn't greatly care.

'I imagine the police have already been to see you about Young's disappearance?' he asked casually.

Mr. Creedy sighed. 'Yes, but I'm afraid I wasn't much help to them. I had to tell Superintendent Manton that I was as much in the dark as anyone. You probably won't

97

credit this, Mr. Cape, but Young walked out of court and out of the building without so much as a word of thanks either to Mr. Imrey or myself. And I haven't seen or heard of him since.'

There was a silence. Then as though the thought had suddenly occurred to him, Adam said, 'Oh yes, I remember something I was going to ask you. There was a chap in court during the Young case whose face was vaguely familiar but for the life of me I can't remember his name.' Mr. Creedy looked attentive. 'I saw you talking together during one of the adjournments. Have you any idea who I mean? A tall chap.'

'Roger Winslow?'

Adam furrowed his brow. 'I suppose it might have been, except that the name doesn't mean anything to me. What's he do?'

'He's in the motor trade.'

'Well, I'm sure I've met him somewhere before. Does he have an attractive wife?'

'He's not married.'

Adam was aware that Mr. Creedy was watching him closely and hoped that he hadn't aroused his suspicions. At the moment, however, he had learnt nothing about Winslow that he didn't already know, and the question was, should he probe further?

'He's a client of mine', Mr. Creedy explained, his eyes steadily fixed on Adam's face. 'I'd promised to take him to the Old Bailey next time I had a case there and it happened to be the Young one.'

Adam blushed, realizing that he must have made his interest too obvious. On the other hand, his own suspicions were aroused by the very deliberate way in which Mr. Creedy had put a full stop to his questions, and he was now more than ever eager to pursue his own inquiries further.

A few minutes later they parted company and Adam returned to chambers.

There was a message asking him to phone Manton, which he did immediately.

'I'm sorry I haven't been in touch with you before, sir,' Manton said as soon as they were connected, 'but I've informed my superiors of what you told me the other evening and they'd be glad if you'd keep silent about the whole matter.' He paused and when Adam made no reply went on, 'Anyway, sir, I imagine that suits you too, as I don't suppose you want it breezed about the Temple.'

'How's the inquiry going?' Adam asked, pretending not to notice that Manton was in effect blackmailing him into silence.

'Making headway.'

'Any news of Young?'

'No, but there will be soon.'

'You sound confident.'

'One has need to on this job.'

'I was talking to Young's solicitor just now.'

'Mr. Creedy?'

'Yes. He told me he hasn't been able to help you.'

'We never expect Mr. Creedy to help us unless it suits him.'

'You think he may be hiding something?'

'What makes you suggest that?' Manton asked sharply.

'I'm sorry, I thought you were suggesting it, Superintendent.'

There was a brief pause, before Manton said, 'I must ring off now. Don't forget what I said about keeping silent, sir; and you won't do any more amateur sleuthing, will you?'

'What do you mean?' Adam asked guiltily.

'Wasn't it you making inquiries at Young's place of work on Saturday morning? It sounded like you from the description.'

'Yes, it was.'

'Lay off it then, sir, and leave us to get on with the job. We'll certainly let you know when we need your help, and I don't mean that sarcastically because we may want it in due course. But till then, stick to barristering, will you, sir? I'm sure your Benchers would prefer it.'

Before Adam could make any reply to this veiled threat to report him to the Benchers of his Inn of Court, Manton had rung off. When, an hour later, he went across to lunch in Hall, he looked at the row of elders sitting at high table who formed the Benchers of his Inn and pictured himself facing them under somewhat different circumstances, for despite Manton's warning, he was quietly determined to continue his own investigation. He had come to feel that he owed it to the memory of Carole Young, not to mention to his own conscience.

Accordingly, after supper that evening, he set off to make a reconnaissance of Winslow Motors, though with no clear idea of what might be achieved. The project was made easier by the fact that Sara had had to accompany an aunt to the theatre.

Light was fading when Adam alighted from a bus at Shepherd's Bush. The temperature had dropped and he was thankful for the raincoat he'd decided to put on for the expedition. Moreover, it gave him an aura of anonymity.

Only one week to go to August bank holiday and the greatest holiday exodus of the year. It could still be a tropical week-end, though oilskins and winter woollens seemed the more likely garb at the moment. So much for the charm of uncertainty of the English weather.

A quarter of an hour's walk brought him to Winslow Motors, whose neon sign he spotted from some distance away.

The main showroom was bright with spotlights trained on to a scarlet Austin Healey gleaming in the centre of the floor. Adam gazed at it with envy and admiration. Trouble was that if he ever had enough money to buy such a car, he probably wouldn't want it anyway, preferring by that time something more staid in appearance.

As far as he could see, the premises consisted of a single-story building of which the showroom was the front half. A door at the back presumably led to offices and possibly a workshop. On the left of the building, as one faced it, was a yard, full of second-hand cars, which was surrounded by a high wire fence and which was also floodlit. The yard was 'L' shaped and extended round the back of the building.

There appeared to be no one about and Adam was wondering what he should do next, when he heard sounds of faint movement at the rear of the yard. Diving quickly into shadow he peered between the cars to try and see what was happening. He heard a door being softly closed. There was the click of a lock and a few seconds later, a figure moved quickly and silently across the far side of the yard.

It was almost too late before he realized that there was an

exit from the yard in the far left-hand corner which led into a lane running parallel to the road he was in.

Adam left his hiding-place in the shadows and after only a second's indecision ran with heart pounding towards the turning which he surmised must connect the two streets. A courting couple in a doorway stared after him in surprise and a dog joined him, racing enthusiastically along at his side.

As he approached the corner, he saw the lights of a car and shrank abruptly back against a dark shop-front so as not to be seen. The dog, disappointed by the change of plan, barked at him encouragingly.

Adam made a dive at it at the same moment as the car appeared and turned left.

A second later, it passed him accelerating hard in the direction of Shepherd's Bush and he released the wriggling animal which gave him a final affronted bark and ran off.

He felt certain that the driver of the car had not noticed him, though he, Adam, had had no difficulty in recognizing the driver.

It had been the tough, barrel-chested man he had seen on Saturday morning in the tobacconist's opposite Mather Brothers.

CHAPTER TEN

A
S HE SAT in a bus going down Holland Road, Adam
tried to fit this latest piece of the puzzle into place.
It was clear that there was a connexion between
the tough man and Winslow. Winslow had attended
Young's trial and the tough man had been nosing around
the area where Young had worked. But what did that
indicate and how was it related to Young's disappearance
and Carole Young's murder? Certainly the tough man
looked capable of murdering anyone.

It was only as he was getting off the bus that it suddenly
occurred to him to wonder what the tough man had been
doing at all at Roger Winslow's car premises at that hour of
the evening. Hardly selling cars, and he certainly bore no
resemblance to an office clerk who had been working late.
So what had he been doing there?

There was only one way to find out and that was to make
a further reconnaissance the following evening. Adam was
surprised at the ease with which he accepted this prospect.
Almost gone was the apprehension which had filled him on
his first evening's prowl when he had gone to the Youngs'
house in Warren Place.

He was still trying to make sense out of the pieces of
information in his possession when he arrived back at his

lodgings. It was shortly before eleven o'clock and he decided to go to bed.

As he undressed, it suddenly occurred to him to wonder who had paid for Young's defence. Could it have been Winslow? This would have accounted for his presence in court, and also for the fact that Mr. Creedy had been his solicitor. But even if this was a correct deduction, it still left the mystery of Carole Young's death unanswered and it failed to explain why Winslow had acted as he had. Altruism or philanthropy seemed equally unlikely motives for his conduct.

Puzzled, intrigued and determined to probe further, Adam went to sleep and dreamt of Debbie.

It was a dream from which he awoke with a start, and as he turned over on his other side he murmured a rueful apology to Sara.

The last week in July and the Temple was like a sea-side hotel at the close of the season.

As the most junior member of chambers, Adam had been told by William that he ought to remain on hand during August and not go on holiday until Charles Imrey returned at the end of the month. Moreover, as William had reminded him, the courts in which he was most likely to be required to appear, namely County Courts and Magistrates' Courts, did not shut down for the long vacation.

Accordingly on the day following his latest venture in detection, Adam turned up at chambers at the usual time, but, on finding no work to do, told William that he was going to retire to the Inn's library where he could be found if occasion arose.

It didn't arise until the afternoon when, considerably to his surprise, having regard to recent events, another brief arrived for him from the Yard. He was called to the library telephone and immediately recognized William's prim tones.

'You'd better come back, sir.'

'What's happened?'

He could almost see the faint smile on his clerk's face as William replied, 'A brief has come for you from the Solicitor's Department at the Yard. Housebreaking at Lambeth the day after tomorrow.'

This was not a cryptic reference to an impending crime at the Archbishop's residence, but telegraphic jargon to describe a case of housebreaking to be heard at Lambeth Magistrates' Court.

'I suppose I'd better come back and read it.'

'It's quite short and looks perfectly straightforward, sir.'

'I'm sure it must be to be wafted my way.'

It proved to be as William had stated and in less than half an hour Adam felt he knew as much about the case as he ever could. Nevertheless he was gratified at receiving the brief and could only assume that Manton's warnings had not been translated into sanctions on the professional plane. He was relieved too that it wouldn't be necessary to take the papers home for further study, since he had other plans for the evening.

Sara phoned him as he was about to leave chambers and apparently took it for granted that they would be spending the evening together.

Adam agreed to meet her for supper, but said firmly he would have to return home early as he had a new brief to read. Sara was suitably impressed by this piece of news and

Adam, as a token salve to his conscience, took the brief home after all.

It was a few minutes after half past nine when he gave Sara a warm good-night kiss – the warmer to make up for his deception – and headed for Winslow Motors.

The scarlet Austin Healey stood gleaming as before in the centre of the show-room, and well polished second-hand cars still filled the yard at the side of the main premises.

But scarcely pausing, Adam walked on to the turning from which the tough man had emerged in his car the previous evening.

As he had surmised, it was a short street connecting the main road with the lane which ran at the rear of the properties. It was bounded on each side by a high wooden fence.

Adam gave a backward glance at the friendly normality of the main road and then with quickening excitement dived into the dark street, his eyes firmly fixed on the lamp at the end, which cast a wavering light. It was like going up to bed in the dark as a child and never being certain what evil thing might not be lurking in the shadows. It was always with relief that he used to reach the sanctuary of his bedroom where Ada, their old negress maid, had left a nightlight.

He reached the lane and paused in the shadow of the fence to regain his breath before going farther. A furtive look confirmed that it was no more than a service track for the various properties in the main road which backed on to it. The surface was cinder and a number of cars were parked along its length. Otherwise it was deserted.

Adam crept round the corner and hugging the fence

reached the rear entrance to Winslow Motors' yard. There was a double wooden gate with a wicket door in the left panel. He gave it a tentative push and it swung open. A moment later he had stepped inside and was cowering in the shadow of a breakdown vehicle.

Through the lines of vehicles he could see the lights of the main road which ran at the far side and their sight made him feel more confident.

'Well, Adam Cape, you won't achieve anything by standing beside this old rescue bus all night. So you'd better make a move', he muttered to himself, and keeping in the shadow of the fence moved stealthily along until he was directly behind the rear of the premises.

A row of dark windows and a door faced him. To the left of the door, steps led down to a basement; probably, he surmised, to where the heating plant was installed. The whole place appeared to be in complete darkness and there was no sign of any life. Tough man didn't apparently make a habit of nocturnal visits. So much the better, he would now be able to take a closer look.

With caution born of the state of jitters which still gripped him, he crept towards the building, dodging for cover from car to car. Finally he stood in the shadow of its very wall, peering down into the small concreted area from which basement steps reached up to ground level.

He could see a door, also a window which was blacked out by a sheet of cardboard.

It was while he stood there listening to his own pounding heart beats that he was suddenly certain that he heard a faint movement behind the basement door. A few seconds later it was repeated.

With sweat pouring off him, he tiptoed to the top of the steps.

Six steps, a door and what?

He was about to descend when he experienced a sledge-hammer blow on the back of his head and felt himself hurtling into roaring blackness. Then he knew nothing more.

CHAPTER ELEVEN

A DAM opened his eyes and quickly closed them again as a searing pain exploded in his head.

He felt sick, terribly sick, and yet he dared not move. Indeed, he was convinced that his very life depended on complete immobility. Not merely because the pain of any movement was so excruciating, but because, somehow, he knew it was vital for him to decide on a course of action before his captors saw that he had regained consciousness.

He wondered where he was; in what squalid attic or cellar he was being held prisoner.

Instinct told him that his hands and legs were likely to be bound and that he was almost certainly gagged. To discover these things when your mind seems wholly disconnected from the numbly throbbing flesh which is your body is easier said than done.

With laborious effort he slowly moved his tongue round his mouth and reached the conclusion that he was not gagged after all. Next he tried his arms and legs, an operation which was rather like talking long-distance on a particularly bad connexion. Eventually, however, he was satisfied that all his limbs were free. Moreover, in the course of this discovery he realized something else, namely that he was tucked up in bed.

He decided to risk opening his eyes again and found himself looking into the pretty face of a hospital nurse.

'I thought I saw you moving just now', she said. 'How do you feel?'

'Terrible.'

'Head?'

'Splitting.'

'It'll pass, but you must have absolute rest for the next twenty-four hours.'

'Where am I?'

'Bayswater General Hospital.'

'What time is it? What day?'

'It's breakfast-time on Wednesday morning.'

Adam tried to work this out but the effort made him wince.

'How long have I been here?'

'You were brought in just before midnight.'

A new voice now broke in, a male one. 'Hello, nurse, come round, has he?'

Adam rolled his eyes to see a white-coated young doctor standing at the other side of the bed. 'Lucky you've got a reasonably thick skull, Mr. Cape. As it is, there are no fractures and you should make a complete recovery in a few days. Now you must rest.'

'Who brought me here?'

'The police found you.'

'The police?'

The young house surgeon nodded. 'But no more questions now. There'll be time for those later.'

'But I must . . .' But the effort of trying to collect his thoughts was too much and with a groan he closed his eyes. Perhaps if he lay quite still, he'd be able to think straight.

When he next awoke, he felt very much better, despite a continuing headache. The room was empty and after feeble attempts to find his wrist-watch, he rang the bell which was pinned to the sheet.

It was answered by the same nurse he had seen before.

'Hello', she said, with a professionally bright smile. 'Feeling better?'

'Yes. I can't find my watch.'

'I don't think I've seen it around. They probably took that as well.'

It seemed a curious answer but Adam hadn't the strength to pursue the matter. 'What time is it?'

'Nearly four o'clock.'

'Same day?'

'Yes, you've been asleep for over seven hours. I'll go and tell the doctor you're awake. It's for him to decide if you can see visitors.'

'Do you mean someone's waiting?'

'Miss Sloman is and the police wanted to know as soon as you were fit enough to be interviewed.'

Five minutes later, after the doctor had come and gone again, Sara was ushered in.

'Only a few minutes, mind, and don't excite him', the nurse admonished as she left them together.

'Oh, Adam!' Her eyes were glistening and as she bent over to kiss him lightly, a tear fell on to his forehead. 'Oh, Adam!' She turned away and blew her nose.

'I'm all right now', he said with a fragile smile. 'But how did you know I was here?'

111

'It was in the stop-press of the morning papers.'

'In the papers!'

'There's more in the later editions.'

'What do they say?'

'How you were beaten up and left unconscious in the gutter.'

Adam's mind still felt as if it was clogged with thick treacle.

'In the gutter?' he asked after a pensive pause. 'What gutter?'

'I suppose you don't remember anything of what happened', Sara replied, gazing at him with yearning.

'Not much. What did happen?'

'The police say you were obviously attacked from behind, as you were walking along the street, and then robbed as you lay unconscious.'

'Robbed?'

'They took your wallet and your watch. Do you remember how much money you had on you last night?'

'Three or four pounds only.'

'You never saw them come up on you?'

'Who?'

'The men who attacked you.'

'Was there more than one then?'

'I thought they always worked in gangs in those parts.'

Adam closed his eyes. The whole thing seemed to be getting out of hand. Gangs! Streets! Robbers!

'Where exactly was I found?' he asked wearily.

'In Blanchard Street.'

'Where's that?'

'Notting Hill. Oh, Adam, what were you doing there?

You told me you had to go home and work. Why couldn't you have told me you were going out somewhere?'

So he had been picked up unconscious in Notting Hill. No wonder Sara wanted to know what he had been doing there. He would like to know himself.

She spoke again, this time in a conspiratorial whisper. 'Did you go there in connexion with the Young affair? Have you found out something? That's what Tony thinks.'

'Tony? How does he come into it?'

'He phoned me as soon as he'd read about it in the papers. He was terribly upset. He's coming to see you as soon as you're well enough.' There was a silence in which she caressed his hand. 'Don't you remember at all, Adam, why you went to Blanchard Street last night?'

Adam shook his head dully. It was all too difficult to fit together and try and make sense of. At the moment all he knew was that he had never been near Blanchard Street in his life, but that the effort of explaining this to Sara was beyond him.

The nurse came bustling in and with a smile indicated to Sara that she should leave.

'You can come and see him again tomorrow.'

Adam closed his eyes and lay back exhausted while the nurse fussed about him.

She completed her chores and was about to slip out of the room when he suddenly raised himself up and said with compelling urgency, 'Tell Superintendent Manton I must see him; now, immediately.'

CHAPTER TWELVE

Soon after the nurse had departed, the young house surgeon came back.

'You can't have any more visitors today. Tomorrow, perhaps, if you get some proper rest.'

'But I must see the police now', Adam said helplessly. 'It's terribly important.'

'Nothing's as important as your having rest. If you start exciting yourself, you're going to be here much longer than if you do as you're told like a good chap. The police know you were beaten up. They're doing their best to find out who did it, so you just forget about everything and rest. Or we shall have to make you rest.'

Adam sighed – a sigh of infinite weariness. 'Tell Superintendent Manton,' he said with bleak despair, 'that I can help him solve the Young case.' Making a great effort to rivet the doctor's attention, he went on, 'Tell him that I know something.'

He had no idea how much time passed before he was aware of soft movements in his room and opened his eyes to see Manton studying him from the foot of the bed.

'Remember what the doctor said.' Manton nodded as the nurse, who had whispered this, melted out of the room.

'You have something you want to tell me, Mr. Cape?'

Adam could detect a note of suspicion in Manton's tone, and realized that it would be past his strength to try and persuade him of the truth if he showed any disinclination to accept it. Once he had told him everything, it would be up to Manton what use he made of the information. He, Adam, would have done his best and could drift back into unconsciousness.

'I know where Young's being held . . . in the basement of a garage near the White City . . . Winslow Motors.'

He had the satisfaction of seeing a spark of interest in Manton's eyes.

'You saw him there?' Manton asked quietly.

Adam shook his head and immediately screwed up his eyes with pain.

'But I'm sure.'

'How?'

'That was where I got knocked out. I was never in Blanchard Street. They must have dumped me there – afterwards.'

Manton pursed his lips, and looked thoughtful. Then he refocused his gaze on Adam's face which was pale and drawn against the expanse of white pillow. 'But how do you know Young is at this place . . . this garage . . . if you haven't actually seen him?'

'I'm certain he is.'

'As a result of your own investigations?' Manton's bright blue eyes rested coldly on Adam as he spoke.

'Yes.'

'Was it Young who coshed you?'

'No, no.'

'Who did?'

'It must have been a big, tough-looking man I'd seen there the previous night.'

'And you saw him there again last night?'

'No, but . . . but I'm sure it was he. It must have been he.'

'Very well, Mr. Cape, I won't trouble you further. The doctor's told me not to tire you, but I shall want a lot more details as soon as you're fit enough for a proper interview.'

There was a steely edge to his tone, but Adam was past caring. His head was again throbbing with fiery waves of pain and he yearned for oblivion. Shortly after Manton's departure, it came.

It was the next morning before he became conscious of the world again, and he awoke feeling hungry, and clear-minded.

He ate his breakfast, and impatiently awaited the doctor's visit, since he wished to ascertain the prospects of discharge.

Before the doctor came, however, he was brought a couple of newspapers to read and was horrified to see the space and prominence given to the affair.

'Beaten-up barrister still unconscious' was the headline in one paper, and the other's ran 'Did Counsel know too much?'

This second one was anything but reassuring and Adam read what followed with a distinct feeling of apprehension. It seemed, however, that the writer of the piece had nothing more in mind than that Adam had recently been connected with a case which had been followed by mysterious happenings. This was, of course, nothing more than newspaper kite-flying to find out whether their deduction was true, as, of course, it was. Nevertheless, it was a warning to him of what lay ahead, for the Press certainly wouldn't rest if there was anything to the story.

A voice broke in on his somewhat gloomy reverie. 'Reading about yourself?' the young doctor asked with a smile as he advanced towards the bed.

'I didn't think they'd have gone to town this much.'

'You underestimate your news value. We've had reporters buzzing round the hospital since you were brought in. Not to mention phone calls from practically every paper except *The Times.*'

Adam gaped. 'But this is terrible!'

The doctor shrugged. 'It's a nuisance, but one we're used to. After all, the very fact that someone is brought in as a casualty invests him with news value. Most people only get their names in the papers if they're knocked down by motorcycles or cut off a finger making sandwiches or electrocute themselves in the bath. Anyway, I gather you're better today.'

Adam nodded. 'When'll I be allowed out?'

'Tomorrow with luck. The X-rays show that you haven't got any fractures, and you haven't developed any post-concussional effects, so I expect we'll let you go home tomorrow or the next day.'

'Is it your decision when I go?'

'No, Dr. Black's. He's the Registrar.'

'I haven't seen him, have I?'

'No, but he's seen you. He'll be looking in later this morning. He was away all yesterday.'

Adam groaned as he thought again of the newspapers' interest in him. 'I suppose I shall have to run the gauntlet of reporters when I am discharged.'

'Oh, don't worry about that. There are a good many exits to this building and if you want to get away unseen, we'll be able to manage it. Anyway, the police may lend a hand.'

'The police?'

'Yes; that superintendent who was here last night said he didn't want the Press to get hold of you, asked us to let him know before you were discharged.'

'Oh', Adam said bleakly, searching for the significance of this.

He felt that he had enough on which to ponder and spent the morning, between the visits of doctors and nurses, staring at the ceiling in deep thought, with his hands clasped beneath his head.

Just as he had finished his lunch, which he was allowed to have sitting in a chair wrapped in a hospital dressing-gown three sizes too large, Sara appeared.

She gave a small exclamation of delight at seeing him up and ran across to kiss him.

'You smell delicious', Adam said. 'It's a change after all the antiseptic odours of this place.'

'You look much better today.'

'I am. I'm fine, or rather I was until I read the news-papers.'

Sara nodded sympathetically. 'Some of them have hinted that you were beaten up because of something to do with the Young case.'

'I know.'

'Were you? I mean' – there was a slight catch in her voice – 'I mean, can you now remember what you were doing in Notting Hill?'

118

Adam pushed out his lower lip and gave a sigh of surrender.

'I was never in Notting Hill', he said, and proceeded to tell her everything.

'The police should have found Young by now then', she said excitedly when he had finished.

Adam nodded. 'Provided he *was* hiding there.' He paused. 'I'm certain he was. I definitely heard sounds of movement in the basement at the rear. And it would explain the tough-looking man being on Winslow's premises at that hour. He was obviously Young's keeper. After all, Young couldn't go out and show his face, so someone had to bring him food and look after his needs.'

'But what do you think is the connexion between Young and Winslow?'

'I've been trying to think of an answer to that for the past three days, but I'm no further forward.'

'And why should Winslow want to hide him?'

'Same question, same answer', Adam replied with a shrug. 'Anyway, I've now passed the ball to the police and it's their problem.'

Sara glanced at her watch and sprang off the bed on which she had been perching.

'It's after two, I must fly or I shall get the sack. Good-bye, Adam darling. I'll look in again this evening. Oh, good heavens, I nearly forgot. I brought you this. It's a cable; I imagine, from your parents. I picked it up at Miss Brown's.' She rummaged in her bag and handed Adam a crumpled envelope, and watched him while he opened it. 'Do they sound terribly worried? Shall I send a reply for you?'

Adam sighed. 'They've read something in the local rag.

But don't wait now. I'll concoct a reply before you come back and you can send it off on your way home.'

Sara fled and a little later, despite his protests, Adam was put back to bed and told to rest. To his surprise he felt himself drifting off to sleep.

When he awoke, tea and another visitor arrived at one and the same moment.

'Hello, Adam, you snake in the grass', Tony Lelaker greeted him from the door.

Adam grinned. 'Come on in and hand over your gift.'

'What gift?'

'You mean to say you've come to visit a sick friend without bringing a gift? No grapes? No half bottle of gin?'

'You're jolly lucky I haven't brought a mallet to give you another belt over the head.' His expression became reproachful. 'But honestly, Adam, fancy going off and doing all this without a word to any of your friends, in particular to Sara and myself.'

'How do you know what I've been doing?' Adam asked suspiciously.

'I spoke to Sara on the phone this afternoon. She told me what you'd been up to.' Observing Adam's expression, he went on quickly, 'But don't worry, despite your unfriendly behaviour, mum's still the word. I shan't give any handouts to the Press.'

'You haven't brought a midday paper by any chance?'

''Fraid not, but there was nothing about Young having been found.'

Adam bit his lip. 'The police mightn't wish to advertise the fact yet, I suppose.'

'Either that or he mayn't have been hiding there after

all.' Tony lit a cigarette. 'Sara told me about the toughie you saw at Winslow's premises and how you'd also seen him in a shop opposite where Young used to work.'

'That's right.'

'I wonder what the connexion there is. Haven't you any ideas for me to work on?'

'For you to work on?'

'Sure. Don't you see, Adam, now they've cottoned on to you, you won't be able to do any more, you'll have to retire from the fray, or at least give the appearance of doing so, but they don't know who I am and I can take over where you left off.'

Tony Lelaker's eyes shone hopefully and eagerly and Adam felt brutal when he replied, 'Sorry, Tony, I've already handed on the baton – to the police.'

Lelaker shook his head sadly. 'To think that this is the same Adam Cape I was at school with.'

'You seem to forget that I've recently been knocked out and darn near killed. Just bear that in mind before you start reproaching me for being unadventurous.'

Lelaker's face broke into a grin. 'It's sheer envy on my part, Adam. I apologize. I think you're terrific, a cross between the Saint, the Four Just Men and Robin Hood.' He sighed and said reflectively, 'It still seems pretty obvious that Young murdered his wife, but why should Winslow have given him shelter? That's what I can't follow.'

'And assuming I'm right about it, why did he pay for his defence?'

'Winslow must be under some sort of obligation to Young. Perhaps Young's blackmailing him. I know, perhaps there was a tie-up between Winslow and Carole Young.'

121

'Could be. But stop it, Tony. If there was a tie-up, let the police find out.'

'I wonder if they know any more than you do?'

'I couldn't say. All I do know is that I'm not very popular with them.'

'But you've done hellish well, Adam, to find out as much as you have. They ought to be very grateful to you.'

'How's Debbie?' Adam asked in an effort to steer Lelaker's thoughts into another channel.

'She's fine. Sent you her love. She likes you.'

'Most girls do', Adam replied complacently, and yawned.

They exchanged flippancies for a few more minutes and then Lelaker left.

Thinking things over, Adam decided that he would probably have retailed events to Tony in any case, even if Sara had not done so first. He knew he could trust them both not to spread the news too broadly. Nevertheless, he hoped that Manton would not find out that he had been talking, seeing that he had been particularly adjured not to.

He had hardly thought of Manton, when the Superintendent appeared in person.

'I gather you've recovered, Mr. Cape', he said in an expressionless tone. 'Sister tells me you'll probably be discharged tomorrow.'

'Young,' Adam asked impatiently, 'have you found him?'

'That's what I've come to see you about', Manton replied evenly, as he tossed his hat on to the foot of the bed. 'No, we have not found him.'

'You mean that he wasn't hiding at Winslow Motors?'

'Exactly, Mr. Cape. Not only was he not there, but there was no sign of his ever having been there.'

Adam was dismayed by the bleakness of Manton's news. What could he say now? All that he had apparently achieved was to increase Manton's suspicion of him. Indeed, the look which was being projected at him bore none of the solicitude of the ordinary hospital visitor.

'But I'm certain there was someone in the basement. I heard movement.'

'Mr. Winslow keeps chinchillas, Mr. Cape. There are four of them in a cage down there. They do a lot of running about.'

'But who on earth ever heard of chinchillas being kept in the basement of a motor-car show-room?'

'It's warm down there.'

'But chinchillas and cars don't mix!'

'You may not know it – I didn't until today – but a lot of people keep chinchillas these days. They buy them as an investment and hope to get rich quick when the creatures start multiplying, which, I'm told, they usually do, provided you've got them the right sexes.'

'Is this what Winslow himself told you?'

'It's what I've found out.'

Adam noticed the slight hesitation which preceded Manton's reply. 'Have you been able to find out anything about Winslow?'

'Only that he's a respectable man of business, Mr. Cape.'

'Then what was he doing attending Young's trial, and why did he show such an interest in the case?'

'Look, Mr. Cape, you told me yourself that he came to the Old Bailey as a friend of Mr. Creedy's, and as far as I'm aware he showed no more interest in the case than anyone else who happened to be there. Don't you think it's time that you tried to control your lively imagination and ceased making a nuisance of yourself to the police?'

Adam flushed. 'It wasn't a lively imagination that produced a lump on my head', he said witheringly. 'Can Winslow explain how I got from his premises to the street in Notting Hill where I was found unconscious?'

'At the moment Mr. Winslow is not called upon to explain anything. The position is that you have failed to make out your case against him, and I am left wondering, Mr. Cape, exactly what to think about you.'

His tone was biting and left Adam burning with resentment.

'I take it then,' he said with mustered dignity, 'that you don't even believe I was knocked out at Winslow's place, that I was ever there in fact?'

'If you were there, Mr. Cape, you were clearly on private premises where you had no right to be.' He picked up his hat and stood fingering the brim, apparently undecided whether to say something further. 'I make no apologies for having been brutal, and I give you no guarantee that I shan't be more so.' He turned and a second later Adam was left alone to nurse his feelings.

He was certainly in no mood to receive, half an hour later, his next visitor, who turned out to be Charles Imrey.

'Hello, Adam, thought I'd drop in and bring you chambers' wishes for your speedy recovery.' Standing in the middle of the room with umbrella in one hand and bowler hat in the other, he gazed at Adam with an air of detached condescension. 'Must say you don't look too bad. When are they going to let you out?'

'Probably tomorrow.'

124

'So soon. I remember when my brother-in-law had con-
cussion, he behaved very oddly for some time afterwards.
Aren't they afraid you may develop delayed symptoms?'

'Apparently not.'

'Well, that's fine, we'll look forward to having you back
with us sooner than we'd expected. Incidentally, William
asked me to tell you he'd had to return your Lambeth case,
but not to worry, he was sure the Yard would remember you
when you got back.'

'I'm sure they will too,' Adam said, 'though not quite the
way William means.'

'You've become quite a notorious figure, Adam. I wonder
how it'll affect your practice. On the whole the better
solicitors tend to fight shy of Counsel who've courted
publicity in their private lives, but let's hope that doesn't
happen in your case.' He gave an indulgent laugh. 'After
all, it'd be rather unfair that you should suffer as a result of
being beaten up by footpads.'

It was clear that Charles Imrey accepted the face value of
events and Adam was thankful for this as he had no wish to
become involved in further speculation about the Young
case. Moreover, if Imrey should learn the truth of what had
happened, he would quite likely move for Adam's prompt
expulsion from chambers. Conduct so hideously unprofessional would in his view certainly merit immediate
excommunication.

To Adam's dismay, Imrey now disposed of his hat and
umbrella and sat down, apparently unaware that a pro-
tracted visit would not be welcome. 'I had a rather interesting point taken against me in the Court of Criminal Appeal
yesterday', he said expansively, and ignoring Adam's glazed

expression went on, 'You remember the decision in Ingram's case . . .' Adam's mind drifted away. '. . . Court said credit can be obtained in incurring a liability to pay not only . . .' This is just splendid for a bumped head, Adam reflected savagely. '. . . Of course I argued that on my facts there was never any question of money's-worth and that R. *v.* Jones . . .' The voice droned on and Adam was filled with an obsessive urge to make some profane comment. '. . . in the end they gave judgement in my favour, and I shouldn't be surprised if the case doesn't find its way into the law reports. Rather an interesting point, don't you think? Personally, I never have been able to follow the Court's reasoning in the other case.'

Adam nodded and said quickly in the pause, that followed, 'If you don't mind, Charles . . . I'm a bit exhausted. . . . It was awfully good of you to come.'

'Not a bit. I know one's always glad to have visitors when one's in hospital. A breath of the outside world helps restore the patient's sense of perspective, I always think.' He picked up his things. 'Be seeing you in a day or so, then. Meanwhile, I'll tell everyone you're looking fine and are none the worse for what's happened.'

Adam lay back and closed his eyes. At the moment life seemed in one hell of a mess.

CHAPTER THIRTEEN

A T ABOUT the same time the next morning that Adam
was being smuggled out of a side entrance of the
hospital into a waiting taxi, Detective-Superintendent
Manton was sitting in the ante-room of the Assistant Commissioner (Crime) at Scotland Yard.

There was a short buzz and his personal assistant looked
across at Manton and nodded in the direction of the door
which led into A.C.C.'s room. 'He'll see you now.'

' 'Morning, Manton. Come in and sit down.' The A.C.C.
said briskly from behind his large desk, 'Now then, about
this fellow Cape, what are we going to do?'

'I feel we must do something, sir, if he's not going to
wreck everything for us. I tried to persuade the hospital to
keep him for another week but they wouldn't have it.
Shortage of beds and all that.'

'Anyway, I'm not sure that wouldn't be letting him off a
bit lightly. There isn't only the practical side to it, there's a
principle involved. One can't have young barristers behaving in this quixotic fashion. Our job's difficult enough
without that.' Manton waited and the A.C.C. went on, 'I
know Mr. Justice Dillon quite well. He's the Treasurer of
Cape's Inn and I think I'll have an unofficial word with him,
ask him to give Cape a jolly good talking to and remind
him of a few of his professional responsibilities. One doesn't

127

want to blight the chap's career completely and so I'd sooner not report him officially to his Benchers. On the other hand, it's time he was given a lesson or two.' He paused and gazed thoughtfully out of the window. 'Yes, that's what I'll do. I'll speak to the judge. Probably just catch him before he goes off for the long vacation.'

'Right, sir', Manton said, preparing to be dismissed.

'Still no sign of Young, I suppose?'

'No, sir.'

'Do you think he probably was hiding at Winslow's premises?'

'I wouldn't be surprised, sir. I wish I could have taken a look there myself.'

'I dare say, but I'm sure we were wise not to go barging in. Indeed, I know we were, seeing that Young wasn't there anyway. It was much better getting the Fire Inspector to do a recce for us. No suspicions aroused or anything of that sort. If the police had gone along, on the other hand, we mightn't have learnt anything more and we should certainly have frightened off the birds.'

'True, sir.'

'This fellow, Winslow. Know anything about him? Has he got form?'

'No, not under that name.'

'Well, I suppose we ought to be grateful to young Cape for giving us that lead.'

'Oh, he's certainly helped us in some ways, sir. But equally he could wreck everything if he were to go on. Trouble is one never knows how his type is going to react. If you hand them bouquets, they regard it as encouragement to continue their efforts: if you threaten them, they go on anyway just to see you damned.'

'Well, we'll see if we can't impress him with a few "DANGER" signs this time. By the way, what about the other man whose description he gave you, the tough-looking man? Anything on him?'

'I have an idea, sir, that he might be someone called Gussie Hapgood, who has done quite a number of safe-blowing jobs in his time.'

'Which fits in nicely with your theory?'

'Yes, sir.'

The A.C.C. shifted in his chair, and, recognizing the signal, Manton rose. There was a silence during which the A.C.C. with frowning concentration attempted to balance a silver paper-knife across one finger. After a time, he said, 'We shouldn't lose sight of the fact that we're primarily concerned in solving a case of murder.'

'If I'm correct, sir, the events of the next few days will lead us to Young, and that, I hope, will mean solving the murder.'

'I hope so, too.' He reached for the push-bell on his desk. 'Meanwhile I'll get on the phone to Mr. Justice Dillon and start lighting a fire under Master Cape.'

The day that Adam returned to chambers was stuffily hot and the air was laden with the odours of baked asphalt and diesel fumes. The male population, in particular, looked uncomfortably warm, with its patience beginning to wear thin round the edges.

William greeted him like a son returned from the trenches and the few members of chambers who had not yet gone off on holiday made a point of looking into his room to welcome him back. Though he had been away only three days, it seemed far longer.

Most of them seized the opportunity of expressing stock sentiments and of blaming the abolition of corporal punishment, the dissolution of parental discipline and the understrength of the police for what had befallen Adam. Only Canfield said, with a glint in his eye, 'Remember you've only got one head, Adam. Look after it.'

It was while receiving his colleagues' inquiries after his health that the telephone rang and a voice said:

'This is Kelly, Under-Treasurer. Mr. Justice Dillon would like to see you in the Treasurer's office as soon as possible. He's going away this afternoon. Can you come now?'

'Yes', Adam replied in a hollow tone.

'I'll tell the judge.'

A quarter of an hour later, Adam knocked on the door of the Under-Treasurer, who was the Inn's permanent officer and rather in the nature of the secretary of a club.

'Ah, come in. Sit down, won't you. I'll let Mr. Justice Dillon know you're here.'

'What's he want to see me about?'

'No idea', Kelly replied quickly, so that Adam guessed immediately that he did know. He disappeared out of the room, leaving Adam to his own guess.

It was at least five minutes before he returned and said, 'They'll see you now.'

'They?'

'Oh, yes, I don't think I told you, Sir Alexander Betts is there too.'

Adam tried to recall what he knew of Sir Alexander Betts. He was one of the senior Benchers of the Inn and frequently lunched and dined in Hall. But what else? Was it he who had a thin, purple nose and had been a Colonial Chief Justice or was that Sir Selby Rutter? And if not a Colonial Chief Justice, then what? It was only as he was ushered in to the presence of the two Benchers that he remembered Sir Alexander to be a retired Judge Advocate General of reputed ill-temper.

Mr. Justice Dillon and his fellow Bencher were sitting in large leather chairs on the far side of a table when the Under-Treasurer and Adam entered. They were deep in muttered conversation and it was some time before they looked up. When at length they did so, Kelly said nervously:

'Mr. Cape, my lord.'

'Have a chair, Cape', Mr. Justice Dillon said, indicating one on the opposite side of the table, which faced him and his colleague. Adam sat down and tried to fix his features into an expression of deference and polite interest. 'I expect you have an idea what we want to see you about?'

'I don't think so, Judge.'

Sir Alexander sniffed unpleasantly and Mr. Justice Dillon went on, 'The fact is that we have received a somewhat disturbing report – albeit an unofficial one – of your recent conduct, which seems to have fallen far below that which is expected of a member of our profession. As I say the report is an unofficial one. But it seemed of such gravity that I decided as Treasurer of the Inn that I ought to speak to you about it, since repetition of such conduct would almost certainly lead to formal representations being made to us, and to our then having to consider what action – official action – to take in your case. Do you follow me?'

'Yes, Judge, but may I ask from whom you have received this report?' Adam was surprised at how calm he felt.

Mr. Justice Dillon scratched his ear and Sir Alexander bared his teeth in a grimace.

'You're certainly entitled to be told that', the judge said. 'The Assistant Commissioner of the C.I.D. He says that you've been embarrassing police inquiries by your interference in a certain case. What makes it serious so far as we are concerned is that it appears to be one in which you acted professionally. That so?'

'I suppose it might be seen that way, Judge, but I certainly had no intention of embarrassing the police and I'd like to apologize for having done so. Moreover, the last thing I should ever wish to do would be to traduce my profession.'

He had spoken with a blend of sincerity and contrition which clearly hit the mark with Mr. Justice Dillon, who looked faintly awkward. He was known to be a gentle and kindly man who disliked sentencing prisoners and therefore presumably found his present task equally distasteful, involving, as it did, censuring a member of the profession of which he was inordinately proud.

Sir Alexander cleared his throat and fixed Adam with a gimlet eye.

'Someone wrote once, Cape, that a great advocate's fame is always written in the sand, and he leaves behind him no permanent memorial.' He thrust his head forward. 'I think you want to be careful not to leave behind a memorial – the wrong sort of memorial.' He glowered. 'How long have you been called?'

'Two years.'

'Ever read the late Lord Justice Singleton's book, *Conduct at the Bar*?'

'Yes.'

'I'd read it again if I were you. Remind yourself what the duties of an advocate are.'

Adam returned Sir Alexander's stare with an expression of polite attention. All he could do was sit quietly and accept reproof with outward good grace.

'Once Counsel endorses his brief on conclusion of a case,' Sir Alexander now went on, 'his interest in it has finished, completely finished. It's no part of his duty to adopt the role of private investigator.'

Adam shifted his gaze to the row of portraits on the wall immediately behind his inquisitors. Portraits of late judges of the land, splendid in their judicial robes and with faces which could only belong to men who had been trained to administer centuries of law, trained to uphold the rights of the individual and to ensure that no one, neither sovereign nor parliament nor bureaucratic departments of government, encroached on the basic liberties accorded the humblest citizen.

Maybe the portrait painters had flattered their subjects, had chosen to ignore their lines of weakness. Maybe this was so, but Adam was struck again, as his eye ran along the row of portraits, how each revealed someone to the manner born.

'I see you studying the portraits, Cape', Mr. Justice Dillon said. He gestured towards them with one finger. 'There are some of the men who attained the highest positions in our profession and who cherished its traditions. They indeed were the custodians of civilization; than which, as the late Lord Maugham once said, there can be no higher aim and no nobler duty.' He paused and delicately lacing together his fingers, leant forward in his chair. Adam mentally braced himself. 'Well, Cape, I hope I've sufficiently made my point. All I can do is to urge you to reflect well before undertaking any course of action which might injure the great reputation enjoyed by the Bar.'

'Yes, Judge', Adam said meekly.

'Very well.' He nodded to indicate that the interview was over and Adam rose, gave the two Benchers a small bow and left.

As he walked back to chambers, he reflected on recent events. The trouble was that though he still found it difficult to be repentant, he did, nevertheless, recognize that his behaviour had been grossly unprofessional and deserving of censure by the Benchers of his Inn. But – and this to Adam was the crux of the whole matter – though admittedly unprofessional, he had acted from the best possible motives. Nobody could say he had been moved by self-interest; rather chivalry, and at the worst misguided chivalry.

However, he was ready to call it a day and leave the police to get on with their job, and this he would certainly have done but for a letter waiting for him on his return to chambers. Thus, almost before his resolution had set firm, he found himself once more torn by ambivalence.

When William handed the letter to him, all he noticed before opening it was that the writing on the envelope was unknown to him. The sheet of paper inside was pale blue and scented, and the letter ran :

'Dear Sir,

'I was Carole Young's friend. I'm writing to you because she told me after the case was over that you were the only person at court who was nice to her. She said you looked kind and she felt that you were sorry for her.

'She was on her way home when she dropped in to tell me what had happened. It was the last time I saw her. She was good, sir. He was the bad one in that family. Can't you help clear her name and get justice for her memory ?

'Yours truly,

'Mrs. Doreen Walker.'

The address at the top was 30 Warren Place. This would be five doors from the Youngs' house.

Adam read the letter a second and a third time while his mind wrestled with indecision.

May I speak to you a moment, sir . . . I must talk to someone. Could he ever forget the urgently pleading eyes of Carole Young as she sought his help, only to be spurned ?

And yet despite this, she had apparently told her friend, Mrs. Walker, that he looked kind and had been nice to her.

Adam put the letter in his pocket and gazed thoughtfully out of the window.

There could hardly be anything unprofessional in merely

135

getting in touch with Mrs. Walker and it certainly wouldn't interfere with the police inquiries.

If he did no more than that, neither the A.C.C. nor Mr. Justice Dillon could surely have any cause for complaint. He realized that his mind was already made up.

CHAPTER FOURTEEN

AT WILLIAM'S suggestion he left chambers early that afternoon.

'Don't want to overdo things your first day back, sir', the clerk had said solicitously as he watched Adam sipping a cup of tea, the colour of old brown linoleum. Chambers' tea was brewed by Gregory, the young assistant clerk, who held firmly to the belief that it ought to be drunk very strong and very sweet. Those who disliked sugar in theirs usually now managed to get it without, but there was apparently nothing anyone could do to persuade Gregory to make it less strong. One drank it, and shuddered as one felt the tannin clinging to the inside of the mouth. Nevertheless, such was its obsessive quality that no one ever thought to refuse a cup.

As Adam drank his, he wondered whether he should invite Sara to accompany him to 30 Warren Place. In the end he decided not to, though only because he thought it might inhibit Mrs. Walker to see him arrive on her doorstep with a girl-friend. She might be led to assume, and not without some justification, that he hadn't treated her letter with true seriousness and was merely amusing himself.

It was around five o'clock when Adam arrived in Warren Place and for the first time saw it in daylight. He had to

137

pass number 38 to reach the Walkers' house, but walked by casting it a mere sidelong glance.

He pressed the bell in the middle of the peeling orange front door of number 30 and almost at once heard footsteps in the hall.

'Mrs. Walker?' he asked, when a young woman, wearing a green overall and with her hair in a head-scarf, opened the door.

'Yes, I'm Mrs. Walker', she said, eyeing him suspiciously.

'My name's Adam Cape. I think you wrote me a letter?'

'Oh!' she exclaimed in surprise. 'Yes, I did, but I never expected you to come. I – er – I – won't you come in?'

She was clearly flustered by his visit and still stood staring at him and blocking the doorway for several seconds after extending the invitation. She had protuberant eyes which accentuated her expression of surprise and a full mouth on which she had hastily smeared – or so it appeared – magenta lipstick. She didn't look more than twenty-two or twenty-three.

Adam made a move to enter and she stood aside.

'You'll have to be quick', she said anxiously. 'My husband'll be home in half an hour.'

'Look, Mrs. Walker, I've only come because you wrote to me.'

'I know, but I never expected you to take that much notice of my letter.' Her tone was aggrieved. 'Mr. Walker would be mad if he knew I'd written to you. He doesn't hold with getting mixed up in other people's troubles.' She led the way into a back room which was festooned with drying clothes and went over to a pram in the far corner and peered into it with a worried expression. 'He doesn't like my having the baby but what else could I do? The poor little mite.'

'Is that Mrs. Young's baby?' Adam looked down at the small sleeping form. All he could see was a pair of faintly blue eyelids, a button nose and tiny puckered lips.

'I had to have her, didn't I? Carole's family all live over in Ireland and his . . . well, his wouldn't do anything for her anyway.'

'Why did you write to me?'

'I told you, didn't I? To try and get justice.'

Adam nodded soothingly. He was now more than ever glad that he had come on his own, for it was obvious that Mrs. Walker was extremely nervous at his visit and was probably regretting having written to him.

'Have the police interviewed you?' he asked.

'They've been round a couple of times. That's what started Harry off. I mean Mr. Walker. He said it'd get us all a bad name and we'd have trouble with the neighbours.'

'I don't see why that should happen. It'd be most unfair.'

'Harry says that life is unfair.'

'You knew Carole Young pretty well?'

'She was my friend.' The barriers of hostility erected by her nervousness suddenly came down. 'She was a lovely person, she'd help anyone and she was always bright and cheerful. That is before her husband assaulted her that time. She was quite changed after that. She seemed terribly worried and upset. Frightened, I'd almost say. Several times when I went round I found her crying as she was washing the baby, or doing her housework.' She paused, wrestling to find the right words with which to express herself. 'I swear she was bottling something up. Something happened that she wouldn't tell me about, I'm sure of it. We always used to talk so easy together, but after that knife attack she was different.'

'Did you say so to her?'

'Yes. She just denied it, but I know.'

'Was she fond of her husband?'

'She loved him.' There was something moving about the way she paid this simple tribute – a tribute to both parties, though she intended it only to one.

'At his trial you know, Mrs. Walker, he said that his wife stabbed herself.'

'Sort of stupid lie he would tell to try and get himself out of trouble.'

'You didn't like him?'

'He didn't deserve to have such a good wife.'

'You said in your letter that he was bad. I know he'd been in trouble with the police, but had you something else in mind?'

'He was weak, always getting in with the wrong lot. He didn't like hard work and he couldn't keep money. It went through his fingers like air. She was the housekeeper. Without her, they'd have been in the gutter.'

'Was he fond of her?'

'He always said he was, but how could he have been giving her so much worry?'

'Do you think he killed her?'

'Who else? Of course he did.'

'Why?'

'Because she knew something about him. Like I told you, she was bottling something up.'

'But what?'

140

'How do I know! That's what the police are for, aren't they – to find things out? Not that they seem to be getting very far. Probably can't be overbothered when the likes of us get murdered. Now if it'd been some posh lady . . .'

Adam interrupted her. 'That's not fair or true, Mrs. Walker. I'm quite certain the police are doing all they can to solve the case.'

'Well, why don't they find Frankie Young then? He can't have vanished into thin air.'

'Do you know of anyone who might be hiding him?'

'That's what the police officer asked me. No, I don't. But surely there's something you can do.'

Adam felt embarrassed. 'I'm afraid not, Mrs. Walker.'

'Then what did you come here for?'

'Because you wrote to me', he replied quietly. 'I thought I might be able to help you.'

She studied him for a full minute and then said in a flat, weary tone, 'She said you looked kind, but I suppose you're really just like anyone else.'

There was a sound outside and the door opened and a tall, muscular man with cropped fair hair came in.

'Hi, Rene.' He stopped short as he caught sight of Adam. 'Who . . .' he began when Adam broke in.

'My name's Cape. I'm a barrister and I came to see your wife about the Young case.'

'You working for the police?'

'Not exactly.'

'For Young?'

'No.'

'Whose side are you on then?'

Adam thought fast, and decided there was only one way to avoid being cornered by Mr. Walker's pointed questions.

'My own.' He smiled in self-deprecation. 'I was prosecuting counsel at Young's trial and . . . well, because of something which aroused my curiosity, I've been making one or two inquiries of my own. Quite unofficial mind you, so I'd be grateful if you wouldn't mention the fact to anyone. Particularly not to the police.'

'What did you want to know from my wife?' Walker asked after a pause.

'I knew she was a friend of Mrs. Young's.'

'Who told you that?'

Adam felt that no early Briton could have shown greater suspicion at returning to find a rival in his cave.

'I overheard the police mention it', he said with a placating smile while Mrs. Walker let out an audible sigh of relief.

Walker's brow was furrowed in furious concentration. Suddenly he said, 'Hey, aren't you the chap that was slugged the other night?'

'Unfortunately, yes.'

He turned to his wife. 'Remember my reading you the bit out of the paper, Rene?'

She nodded, and a not unattractive grin broke over her husband's face. 'You live it up, don't you, Mister?'

Adam laughed, with relief at the release of tension. 'I'm the original bungling idiot. I mean I'm constantly getting slugged, though not usually physically.' He observed a frown return to Walker's brow as he sought for the meaning of such flippancies, and went on hastily, 'Well, I mustn't keep you from your meal.' He turned to the girl. 'Thank you very much for seeing me, Mrs. Walker, and answering my questions.'

As he walked back along Warren Place, he tried to assess the value of his visit in terms of fresh information. It was precious little, indeed nothing more than that Doreen Walker was certain Carole Young had some secret bottled up in her after the stabbing incident. Well, maybe that was so, but it was a piece of information of nugatory value.

By the time he reached home, however, he had come to the conclusion that the explanation of everything might, after all, be secreted in Carole Young's sudden change of outlook after her husband's arrest. A change, which, he gathered, was occasioned by something more fundamental than their violent quarrel. Indeed, it appeared that the quarrel was more a symptom than a cause.

What, he wondered, had Frankie and Carole Young quarrelled about?

CHAPTER FIFTEEN

THE next morning Tony Lelaker phoned before Adam left for chambers. It was the Friday before the Bank Holiday week-end and London had been emptying since before dawn.

'What are you doing tomorrow evening, Adam?' he asked breezily.

Adam, however, mistrusted this form of question and parried it.

'Depends on Sara.'

'You're not going out of town?'

'Not till Sunday. Why?'

'I wondered whether you'd like to look after Debbie for me. I'd promised to take her out and now I've got to go and dine with a client up in Hampstead, and she's a bit disappointed. Trouble is, a sizeable deal hinges on my going and I daren't duck out. Debbie understands, bless her, but that doesn't mean she won't be feeling a bit lonely and I wondered if you were free. You seemed to get on rather well together, and I had an idea that Sara was going to her parents for the week-end, so I thought you might be feeling a bit lonely too.'

Adam smiled to himself. He had little doubt who was the instigator of this invitation; Debbie herself. He surmised that an evening out with her probably would be stimulating, as well as prove to be quite an experience.

'I should have enjoyed that, Tony, but I'm afraid Sara wouldn't approve. Actually we're going down to her people in Suffolk on Sunday. She has to work on Saturday morning and we'd made vague arrangements to go out in the evening.'

'Of course, old boy, I wouldn't dream of suggesting you should do otherwise. I'm delighted to hear you're not going to be alone over the week-end. I always feel it's pretty awful being in London on one's own over the public holidays. Anyway, Debbie will just have to lump it for one evening and I'll make it up to her later. Believe me, I'll have to. No further developments, I suppose?'

'Nothing.'

'Must say the police don't seem to get very far with cases these days. I'd feel mighty annoyed if I got bashed on the head and the chap who did it was never caught. Well, have a nice week-end, Adam, and keep out of trouble. Tell Sara not to let you off the lead till she gets you into the country.'

Adam chuckled. 'I'll pass that on. 'Bye Tony.'

''Bye. See you next week.'

Though Adam had used Sara as the reason for decling to escort the glamorous Debbie and had said they had plans to spend the evening together, this was not exactly true. Sara was working in the morning, as he had said, but was spending the rest of the day with a sick girl-friend near Dorking, a fact which he had not mentioned.

The fact was that he had awoken in the middle of the night and in one of those sudden visionary flashes that often come to the wakeful in the still hours had thought he saw, not the solution of the case, but the key to part of it.

He hadn't even been thinking about events, when in his mind's eye there appeared the notice which he had seen pinned to the door of Messrs. Mathers' premises announcing that the firm would be closed for staff holidays from Friday, 2nd August, to Monday, 19th August.

It was in that moment that he felt certain that something was going to happen there, that the next scene in the shadowy drama was destined to be played in the silent wastes of Mathers' printing works.

The more he thought about it, the more certain he became that his hunch was right. A hunch based on the fact that Young had worked there before his trial and that Winslow's muscle-man, as Adam had come to think of him, had been skulking in the neighbourhood on the occasion when Adam had made his own private reconnaissance.

At this juncture, he wriggled into a cooler position in bed to give the matter further thought. It must be that Young had been spirited away in order that he could be used for some purpose – a purpose to be fulfilled in the imminent future and connected in some way with his late employers.

Nocturnal cerebration was not Adam's forte, however, and soon his thoughts had become pleasantly muzzy and receded as they were overtaken by sleep.

It was in a contemplative frame of mind that he concluded his telephone conversation with Tony and left for chambers.

He arrived there to find two surprises. One was a letter from his mother, the other was the presence of Charles Imrey.

'I thought you were driving down to Devonshire today, Charles. William told me last night that you probably wouldn't be in for the next two weeks.'

The corners of Imrey's mouth turned down in an expression of annoyance. Ignoring Adam's remark, he said petulantly, 'Are you going to be in the whole morning?'

'Why do you ask?'

'Are you?' The tone became more grating.

'Yes', Adam said firmly. 'I am.'

If Charles Imrey wanted him out of the way, as his tone seemed to imply, let him explain himself and ask like a reasonable being, instead of behaving with such a sour air of mystery. What had caused him to alter his plans and come into chambers, anyway? Adam sat down and opened his letter. His mother normally wrote only once every two or three weeks and as he had received a letter the previous Monday, he was surprised to see her large bold handwriting on another one so soon.

'Dearest Adam', he read. 'We were shocked to see a paragraph in yesterday's paper describing how you had been attacked in the street by hooligans and left unconscious. Did you get our cable? Are you sure you're all right? The paper today said that you were making a good recovery and had suffered no permanent injury, but our anxieties won't be allayed until we have word from you yourself. I wanted to telephone the hospital but your father said he thought a letter would be less dramatic and that in any event I probably shouldn't get any sense out of anyone. I gather from the newspaper report that all your money was stolen

147

and since the whole episode must have cost you money and more, I enclose a cheque. Do send us word as soon as possible. I hope this particular cloud will turn out to have its silver lining by establishing your name at the Bar.

'With fond love from your ever affectionate,

'Mother.'

There was a laconic postscript in his father's hand which read,

'Your mother speaks for both of us.'

Adam folded the cheque, which was for £100, and slipped it gratefully into his pocket. In sending it, his mother had herself provided the silver lining. He wondered in what manner she foresaw the episode establishing his name at the Bar, though he supposed she had meant his 'reputation'. It had certainly established his name.

Imrey's phone rang. He grabbed the receiver and pressed it tightly against his ear as though afraid that Adam might otherwise overhear. Adam noticed out of the corner of his eye, that his free hand fidgeted nervously with a piece of blotting-paper.

'Hello . . . yes, Imrey speaking . . . er, just hold on a minute . . .' He turned towards Adam. 'Would you *mind, Adam* . . . I have a private call coming through . . .'

For a second Adam hesitated, then getting up with a long-suffering sigh, he walked out of the room to go and wait in the clerk's office.

'I thought Mr. Imrey was supposed not to be coming in today', he observed casually to William.

'I understand that he's now not going down to Devon

148

till *after* the week-end', William replied, and turned hastily to deal with another incoming call on his small exchange.

But for his clerk's presence, Adam would have been tempted to listen in to Charles Imrey's conversation. As it was, a full five minutes passed before a faint click indicated that the caller had rung off.

Adam returned to the room with his curiosity thoroughly aroused, but Imrey didn't even look up as he entered; not that he had expected otherwise.

At lunch-time, they went to the coffee-shop near the Law Courts, which was now firmly identified in Adam's mind with the Young case. During the meal Imrey talked at length and with obvious relish of his battle with the local Borough Council concerning the siting of a street lamp in his road. He had recently knocked them groggy by quoting an obscure section of an obscurer act and could hardly wait to deliver the K.O. with his next letter.

Adam listened fitfully, his own mind being occupied with plans for the next day. It did occur to him, however, that Charles Imrey's mysterious telephone call seemed to have restored him to overbearing good humour.

On the way back to chambers in the afternoon, he dispatched a further cable to his parents, assuring them that he was well and promising an immediate letter, which he wrote during the afternoon.

William came in twice, once to bring him a brief to appear at a magistrates' court on behalf of a wife who was summonsing her husband for maintenance and once to hand him a cheque for fifteen guineas from the Metropolitan Police for his services in the Queen against Frankie Young.

Altogether it was a most satisfactory afternoon, and Adam

took special pleasure in Charles Imrey's reaction to both events, which had been to prick his ears hopefully at William's entrance and then pretend to be completely pre-occupied with his own work when the clerk went across to Adam.

'You'll be in on Tuesday, won't you, sir?' he said as he was about to leave the room after delivering the cheque.

'I'd sooner say Wednesday', Adam replied. 'I'm going down to Suffolk on Sunday and wasn't planning to come back to town till Tuesday evening.'

William pursed his lips doubtfully.

'It'll mean that only Mr. Osgood is in chambers on Tuesday if you're not here, and you never know, sir . . .'

'I should really still be convalescing, you know, William', Adam said in a wheedling tone.

'All right, sir. I'll expect you on Wednesday. If anything urgent comes in on Tuesday requiring you to be in court the next day, I'll have it delivered at your address.'

'Fine', Adam said, relieved and certain that nothing would. Barristers' clerks suffered from the occupational disease of expecting the worst to happen at the least opportune moment. The trouble was that it sometimes did.

He spent the evening with Sara, who still regarded him as something rather fragile after his misadventure.

'What are you going to do tomorrow afternoon and evening?' she asked, as they sat outside a near-by pub drinking. 'You could come down to Dorking with me if you liked, but I don't suppose you would.'

'I'll be all right.'

'You're not going to do any more detective work, are you?'

'I might.'

'I thought you would', she said half excitedly, half anxiously. 'But do be careful this time, Adam.'

'Don't worry, I shall be. I shan't go wandering on to enemy territory this time.' A silence fell, then staring into his tankard like a crystal-gazer, he said, 'I know I'm probably daft or worse, but I feel I've got to go on. That wretched woman's face and voice haunt me all the time. If I'd listened to her for a couple of seconds she might still be alive.'

'But that's absurd . . .'

'Maybe it is, and most sensible people would agree with you. I'd agree with you if it were anyone else than myself involved. But this is one of those occasions when no amount of logic or so-called common sense can quell an uneasy conscience. If as a result of all my poking around, I was no further forward, I'd have given up by now. But I have picked up one or two bits of the puzzle. Roger Winslow, for example. Heaven knows what he's up to, but I'm as certain as anyone can be that he's mixed up in it somehow.'

'But the police, Adam, they've made it clear that they don't want you interfering. If they can't find Young and solve the case, how can you?'

'I'm not trying to *solve* it, like a conjurer doing a trick. I have no wish to spring a single-handed surprise on the police and show them up for idiots, even if I could. On the other hand, the police do depend on information brought to them by the public and there's no reason why this particular member of the public shouldn't work a little harder to get it than is usually the case. It's as simple as that.'

'What about the Benchers of your Inn?'

'Better to satisfy one's conscience and alienate the Benchers than the other way round.'

'But you didn't feel as strongly as this at the beginning. I can't understand . . .'

'I know and I don't blame you or the Benchers or the police or anyone.' He paused. Then taking Sara's hand in his, he said with a sudden grin, 'But, look, all I'm going to do this time is walk round the outside of a building rather in the same way as Joshua did the walls of Jericho, except that I shan't be blowing any trumpets. What could be more ordinary?'

'What building?' Sara asked with a worried look.

'Mather Brothers. The printers in Packhorse Road where Young used to work.'

'But why?'

'Because I have a hunch that something's going to happen there.'

'What?'

'I don't know.'

'And supposing something does happen?'

'If I see anything remotely suspicious going on, I shall immediately go and phone the police.'

'Promise?'

'Cross my heart.' He bent down and lightly kissed her hand. 'I'm sure that you'd sooner I spent my evening doing that than doing the other thing which has been suggested to me.' Sara raised a quizzical eyebrow. 'Yes, Tony rang me up this morning and suggested that if I was at a loose end I might like to take Debbie out tomorrow evening.'

'He didn't!'

'He's got to dine with a wealthy client and poor Debbie will be lonely.'

'What did you say?'

Adam's grin widened. 'I said it was a very tempting invitation.'

The soft hand in his seemed suddenly to sprout claws. Sara said, 'You don't really like her, do you, Adam?'

'Not as much as you, anyway', he replied lightly, and smiled because of her momentarily perturbed expression. He got up. 'Come on, let's go and find some food. I'm hungry. I haven't yet got over being starved in hospital.'

The remainder of the evening passed agreeably, though Adam found his mind straying increasingly to what the next day might bring.

The only thing about which he felt certain – though was this more than wishful thinking? – was that the curtain was about to be jerked aside to reveal a fraction more of the darkly hidden truth.

CHAPTER SIXTEEN

Packhorse road on a Saturday afternoon was no more inviting than when Adam had seen it the first time.

He got off the bus at the halt before Mather Brothers and walked nonchalantly in the direction of the printers, pausing a moment to study his simple disguise in the reflection of a shop window.

Sun-glasses and a Henry Higgins hat provided him with a superficially altered appearance and since each was entirely justified by the weather, he did not even feel odd wearing them. The hat, planted on the back of his head, successfully hid his unruly mop of dark hair and the glasses enabled him to observe without appearing to do so.

Long before he reached Mather Brothers he began peering with apparent idle interest into each shop window he passed in order to provide himself with the reason for making an equally lingering study of their premises when he got there.

As he slowly made his way along the street, he hoped that he looked like a boy killing time on his way to meet his girl-friend.

The first thing he observed about Mather Brothers was that the notice announcing that they were closed for summer holidays had been transferred to the heavy outer door which was now firmly shut. The office windows each side of it were also tightly closed, but Adam seemed to recall that they had been on the last occasion and probably were kept permanently so to shut out both noise and dirt.

Anyway, it was unlikely that, if he was going to see anything at all suspicious, it would be in the front of the building on the main road.

He crossed over to the other side and, after a quick look to make sure there were no customers inside, entered the tobacconist's shop in which he had had his first sight of the tough-man who worked for Winslow.

The same old girl shuffled forward from the shadows at the back and looked at him inquiringly.

'Ten Players, please.'

She handed them to him and fumbled in the till for change.

'Looks like being a nice week-end', Adam observed, gazing pointedly out of the door and across at Mather Brothers. 'Though I suppose you don't get much of a holiday.'

'What do I want with a holiday?' The old lady replied with a sniff. 'It's all people thinks about nowadays. Money and holidays.'

'I suppose a good many of your customers are away at the moment. I see the printing works opposite is closed; must make quite a difference to business when there's no one there.'

'Most of them earn good money too', she said, apparently pursuing a line of thought of her own. 'Not that they'll have any by the time they return. They'll have spent the lot on beer for themselves and a few donkey rides for the kids.'

'What about their wives? Won't they get anything?' Adam asked with a grin.

'The crafty ones will; they'll see that they get into their husbands' pockets first.' She cackled with amusement at the picture conjured up in her mind and Adam decided that he wasn't getting very far.

'Is there anyone over there at all?' he asked. 'I have something I want printed and I'd like to leave it if I can.'

'Isn't there a notice on the door saying they're closed?'

'Yes.'

'Well, you can't leave anything, can you, if they're not open?'

'I wondered if there was someone who could accept orders.'

She shook her head and stared at him mistily. 'They're closed.'

Adam nodded his thanks and left her to her own thoughts. There had been little scope for working the conversation round and learning anything useful, though there was probably little to be learnt in any event. It was quite clear that she had not recognized him from his previous visit, though in the circumstances this was hardly a tribute to his disguise.

He walked on for about fifty yards before recrossing the road and taking a turning which he reckoned would lead him to the back of Mather Brothers' premises.

It did so and he found himself in a narrow street bounded on one side by a timber yard and on the other by a twelve-foot brick wall, which enclosed Mathers' own yard.

The big double doors which were set into the wall looked solidly shut. At the side was a small single door on which was pinned a copy of the company's closed-for-holidays notice.

Adam had a strong urge to press the bell beside this door and see what happened.

By the time he had walked as far as Mather Brothers' farther boundary wall and back again, he felt frustrated and filled with a sense of futility.

What on earth had he ever expected to find out by carefully walking round the perimeter of the premises? He might just as well pitch a camp-stool outside the Houses of Parliament in the wild hope of hearing a debate going on inside. But about one thing he was quite determined and that was not to attempt an entry or do anything which would put him on the wrong side of the criminal law.

He leaned against a lonely tree which marked the dividing wall between the timber yard and a neighbouring warehouse, and realized suddenly that the canal ran at the far side of both premises. The same canal, he guessed, from which Carole Young's body had been recovered.

From where he was standing he could just see the outline of its two banks between the piles of timber.

As he peered, a sudden movement within the yard caught his attention. It was no more than a peripheral glimpse of someone slipping from cover to cover.

Adam held his breath and waited, but nothing further stirred. He tried to recapture in his mind's eye exactly what he had seen. A flitting figure, a pair of trousered legs; that had been all. Of the person's face he had seen nothing; the hair he seemed to think, had been dark, or it could have been that he was wearing a hat.

Ten minutes later, he was almost open to persuasion that

he had imagined the whole thing, for there had been no further sign of life from within the timber yard. Indeed the whole neighbourhood appeared to have been evacuated on this particular Saturday afternoon. The only sounds were those in the distance of vehicles passing along the main road.

He moved from the shelter of the tree and came to a small gate, let into the wire mesh surround, which was one of the entrances to the timber yard. The main entrance for vehicles was farther along in the direction from which he had seen the movement.

To his surprise the catch yielded to his touch and the gate opened. After a quick glance to make sure that the road was still deserted and forgetting all his former resolution, he slipped through and dodged quickly behind one of the stacks of timber, where he expelled a long breath and wiped the sweat off his forehead.

If ever there was a perfect setting for hide-and-seek, Adam now found himself in it. Timber stacks twelve to twenty feet high stretched on all sides with narrow runs between them.

Working on the assumption that the person he had seen was most likely to be hiding behind one of the stacks nearest the road, he moved stealthily towards the centre of the yard, in order to avoid coming upon him suddenly round a corner.

From there he chose one of the runs which ran parallel with the road and started to tiptoe down it, pausing at the end of each stack to look each way along the intersecting runs before flitting across to the cover of the next stack.

His progress was slow and several times he broke out into a fresh sweat as he thought he heard someone behind him

and turned sharply to find only that his ears had been playing him tricks.

At length he reached the farther side of the yard. He had
now reconnoitred all the paths which ran from front to rear
and had not seen a trace of anyone. This could only mean
that whoever it was was lurking in one of the lateral runs.
That is, unless he had slipped out while Adam had been
playing grandmother's footsteps inside.

The only thing to do now was to repeat the performance,
this time moving along a run in the direction of the road
instead of parallel with it.

With faltering nerve, and frequent pauses to crouch and
listen, he accomplished this second leg of his reconnaissance
without observing anything further.

As he flattened himself against the last stack in the row,
he felt utterly exhausted. His calf muscles ached from
unaccustomed use and his shirt was soaked through with
perspiration.

Either the man *had* gone or else he was at the rear of the
yard near the canal where Adam had not penetrated.

After a while he decided to work his way down to this
end. He did so and arrived on the bank to gaze with a small
shiver at the still, opaque water.

The man had definitely gone. Adam felt that he must
have caught a glimpse of him if he had still been in the yard.

Whatever he had been doing, his purpose had been
accomplished.

Adam was suddenly seized by an urgent desire to be gone
himself, to be back in the main road where there were cars
and buses and people.

He dived once more down one of the runs and pausing

only at the last stack to satisfy himself that the road outside was deserted ran across the few yards of open ground to the wire mesh gate.

It was locked.

There was no mistaking the fact, a stout padlock now held the door fast. In a spasm of panic, Adam dashed again for cover behind the timber stacks, and straight into the arms of a man who sprang at him as he reached the nearest.

A rough hand was clamped over his mouth and he felt himself being lifted bodily behind one of the stacks. A second man now firmly gripped his legs.

His hat was pulled unceremoniously down over his eyes and he was hauled to his feet, one arm twisted painfully behind his back.

'I wouldn't struggle,' a hard voice said into his ear, 'or this will happen . . .'

Adam let out a cry as his arm received a sharp twist.

'O.K., start walking.'

Though his hat prevented any all-round vision, he was at least able to see his feet and realized that he was being marched down one of the runs in the direction of the canal.

So that was it. They were going to kill him and throw his body into the canal. The scummy water would part and close again and Adam Cape would have disappeared for ever.

He must stall; every second he gained might mean the difference between life and death, for death he was quite certain it would be this time. Winslow and his gang would not let him go a second time.

It required little effort or simulation to go suddenly weak and sink at the knees.

A second later, however, he shot upright with tears of pain stinging his eyes.

'I told you not to try anything', the voice behind him said coldly. 'It wouldn't take much to break this arm.'

Fear, rage and resentment now fused together in Adam's head in one explosive mixture.

'O.K., break my arm, you bastard. Kill me. Only remember that you can still get hanged for capital murder and it'll merely be a matter of time before the police catch up with you and your lousy friends.'

But his captors made no response save to quicken their pace.

'You can tell Winslow that the police know all about him and that he won't be flashing about the country-side in sports cars much longer. The police know that he's been hiding Young, though accessory after the fact to murder will probably be one of the lesser charges they stick on him. You can tell him that as well if I don't have a chance to myself.'

The last few sentences had been punctuated by exhausted grunts as the mad rush of adrenalin through Adam's veins began to subside.

Any moment he expected to be knocked unconscious, and he reflected morosely on the fact that his last view of the world should be of his own feet shuffling along a dusty path.

'In here', the voice behind him said. 'Pick up your feet.'

Adam stumbled forward, suddenly aware that his arm was no longer being held but hanging numbly at his side.

'You again!' The voice which spoke was different but no more friendly than the other.

With his good hand, Adam pushed back his hat and found himself looking into the cold blue eyes of Detective-Superintendent Manton.

CHAPTER SEVENTEEN

'Yes, MR. CAPE, it is me,' he said after a full minute's silence during which they had been staring at each other, Adam incredulously, Manton like a judge dispassionately assessing sentence on the prisoner before him. They were standing in a wooden hut which was obviously used as a sort of office. Through a grime-caked window, Adam could see the canal.

The man who had brought him in still stood by the door. He was a burly individual who gave the appearance of being made of compressed muscle.

Adam tried to turn his arm and winced with pain. Manton noticed and said, with a sardonic glint in his eye, 'This is Detective-Sergeant Mackenzie. He used to be in the Commandos, and has boxed for the Metropolitan Police on many occasions. It's lucky for you that he knows his own strength.'

'Isn't that all splendid!' Adam retorted with angry sarcasm. 'I presume he'll be an inspector any day now, and then perhaps he won't feel so inhibited about breaking a few arms.'

Manton's expression changed abruptly. 'Don't start that tone with us, Mr. Cape. I've already enough to get you imprisoned, disbarred and deported, in that order, so don't try me further.'

'You'll have difficulty deporting me. I happen to be a British subject but I don't expect they teach you geography in the police.'

His tone was as offensive as he could make it and the anger generated by each of them would have been almost sufficient to melt base metal.

But as suddenly their tempers subsided as Manton let out a sigh of hopeless exasperation.

'You certainly are a case.' He gazed at Adam with an almost sad expression. 'Tell me, Mr. Cape, just what makes you go on against all advice, warnings and reason? Why do you do it?'

Adam shot him a wry look and shrugged his shoulders in a gesture of self-deprecation.

'It won't make sense to you, but . . . well, I feel partly responsible for Carole Young's death. She tried to speak to me after her husband's acquittal and I brushed her off and told her, in effect, to take her troubles elsewhere. Maybe she would still have been murdered anyway, even if I had listened to her, but that I can't know. All I do know is that I may have helped someone to an untimely death.'

'It makes perfect sense', Manton said quietly. 'One half of me applauds your integrity as much as the other half deplores your methods.' He fell into silent study of the floor, then looking up, asked, 'What brought you here this afternoon?'

'This *definitely* won't make sense to you. I formed a hunch that something was going to happen over the way at Mather Brothers.'

Manton's eyes narrowed. 'What?'

'I don't know.'

'What gave you the hunch?'

As Adam told him, Manton listened with pursed lips. 'Not a bad piece of deduction', he said when Adam had finished. 'Not bad at all. If you're disbarred, you might consider joining the strong-arm police.' He looked thoughtful again. 'By the way, have you seen anything suspicious?'

'No, only a movement in the timber yard, and I suppose now that must have been one of your chaps.'

'So that's what brought you into this maze?' Adam nodded. 'The question is what to do with you now you are here. Even if you are on the side of the angels – that's the police side by the way, Mr. Cape – I'm reluctant to let you go roaming again. Of course, it might solve the problem if you were to *volunteer* to stay here until I said you could go. How about that?'

'I volunteer . . . on one condition.'

'You're hardly in a position to enforce conditions; nevertheless, let's hear it.'

'You tell me why you're here.'

There was a pause before Manton replied. When he did so, it was in a tone of quiet determination.

'I'm here, Mr. Cape, to forestall a bank robbery and to catch a murderer.'

165

CHAPTER EIGHTEEN

M ANTON walked across the hut and, clearing a corner
of the heavily cluttered desk, sat on it and clasped
his hands across one knee.

'That's what I'm here to do. You see, like you, I also
have a hunch that something's going to happen across the
way tonight. The only difference between us is that I have
more than a shrewd idea what it is.'

'Isn't there a bank next door to Mather Brothers?' Adam
asked, frowning with the effort of recollection.

'Correct, Mr. Cape. A bank which closed at midday and
won't be open again until Tuesday, thus giving anyone
minded to break in, two and a half clear days to do the job.'

'And Mather Brothers are closed for the next fortnight.'

'Precisely.'

'Then you expect them to gain entry into the bank from
Mathers' premises?'

Manton nodded. 'That's my guess.'

'And Young?'

'Unless I'm right off beam, Young has a vital role to play.
Remember he used to be a storeman at Mather Brothers
before his arrest? Well, it's my guess that he discovered
some way of getting into the bank, a disused air shaft, a
weak spot in a wall, a subterranean passage, something of
that sort, and this week-end he's going to lead them in.'

'Who are *they*?'

Manton shrugged. 'Your friend Winslow perhaps. I don't know for certain.'

'Then you do now believe what I told you happened the night I was knocked unconscious.'

'I've been inclined to believe you all along, but I didn't want to encourage you in further efforts at sleuthing. Indeed, I did my best – a pretty indifferent best as it turns out – to discourage you.'

'But if Young discovered some secret way into the bank, why didn't he use it himself?'

'A modern bank robbery requires greater planning than he could manage single-handed. You need equipment for opening safes and strong-rooms, split-second timing with cars, look-out men. It's more like a Commando operation than a sordid crime. That is, until you get caught.'

'Have you got men hiding inside the bank and the printing works?' Adam asked eagerly.

'I've got men everywhere. Too many of them, in fact. There could be real chaos when things begin.' Manton sounded gloomy. 'That printing works is an absolute rabbit warren. I only hope my chaps don't start knocking out each other in the excitement.'

'Do you think that Young murdered his wife?'

'He's got a lot to explain.'

'Why do you think he did it?'

'Do you really need me to answer that, Mr. Cape?'

Adam bit his lip. 'Because she knew something about the plans for the robbery and he couldn't trust her to keep her mouth shut?'

'Fits, doesn't it?'

Adam hung his head and said miserably, 'So I might have saved her life if I had listened to what she wanted to tell me.'

There was a soft knock on the hut door and a young plain-clothes officer came in.

'Someone's just gone past on a bicycle, sir.'

'Anyone we know?' Manton asked.

'Gus Hapgood.'

'That's your tough friend', Manton said, turning to Adam. 'It looks then as though something *is* going to happen. Gone past on a bicycle, has he? Not a bad idea. Nobody ever looks twice at someone on a bicycle. Suppose he was having a preliminary dekko to make sure the coast is clear.'

Adam couldn't somehow visualize his old foe on a bicycle. He would lack poise and sedateness.

'What'll happen next?'

'He'll probably ride past again, from the other direction, in about half an hour's time.'

'And then?'

'Provided they don't get a sniff of anything being wrong, they'll move in as soon as it's dark. They'll reckon to have a clear forty-eight hours.' Manton observed Adam's incredulous expression. 'They could need it too. Despite all the modern burglar's paraphernalia, bank strong-rooms don't always fall apart with the first bang.'

'How long will you give them before you raise the alarm?'

Manton began to reply and then stopped. 'Why am I answering your questions? You're under arrest. Semi-arrest, anyway. For all I know you could even be one of them.'

168

Adam gave a nervous laugh. In the last few minutes he had come to realize how much his immediate future depended on Manton. To placate, not to antagonize, was his aim.

'You know I'm not or you wouldn't have told me as much as you have. As a matter of fact, I'll probably be able to help you when things start.'

'You'll help by stopping right here in this hut. I'm not going to have you getting in the way. Believe me, Mr. Cape, if I could send you back to the station without arousing attention, I would.'

'But I'm the one person who can identify Winslow and Hapgood.'

'There'll be plenty of time to identify them afterwards. We don't go shining torches into people's faces and stop to ask a lot of formal questions on a job like this. If we don't manage to take them completely by surprise, it'll turn into a proper pitched battle. And that'll be no place for you to be.' He looked Adam up and down. 'I know you're quite an athlete and I'm not worried about you for your own sake, I promise you that. No, Mr. Cape, what deters me is all the form-filling there'd be afterwards if you tripped and broke your leg. You're a lawyer, you should know all about civil liability claims. Policemen these days can hardly tell anyone the time without running the risk of being sued.' He paused. 'So that's why you're staying in this timber yard until I say you may leave.'

Adam turned away despondently and looked out of the window. It was still quite light and he supposed nothing would be happening yet. He heard the door open and Detective-Sergeant Mackenzie speak.

'Hapgood's just gone past again, sir.'

'Nothing else?' Manton asked.

'Not yet, sir.'

'O.K. I'm just coming.' Addressing Adam, he said, 'I've a number of things to attend to now, Mr. Cape, so I must leave you for a short while. I know that you'll understand my locking the door.'

As Adam heard the key turn, he blew a derisive raspberry at the closed door, and sat down in the only available chair. He couldn't altogether blame Manton for his attitude, but on the other hand he had no wish to spend the next few hours cooped up in a small hut when exciting events were taking place only a few yards away. Although Manton had declined to answer the question, he nevertheless assumed that the police would spring their trap as soon as the gang was inside, and this would mean that everything should be over by midnight.

He looked at his watch. It was nearly half past nine and dusk was well advanced.

Half an hour later, the door was unlocked and Manton came back in.

'Sorry you have to be in the dark', he said cheerfully.

'Anything happening yet?'

'No.'

'When do you expect them?'

'In the next two or three hours. At any rate before dawn tomorrow.'

'But I thought you said they'd reckon to have forty-eight hours to complete the job.'

'I did, but I could be wrong; wrong about everything, but I hope not.'

'Look, Superintendent, if you don't lock me in, I'll promise to keep out of the way. After all, I have been quite useful to you. I put you on to Winslow and Hapgood, remember.'

'You've also been quite a nuisance to me, Mr. Cape.'

'In what way?'

'A potential nuisance, shall we say?'

'Ha! The fact is that you can't specify a single thing I've done which has hampered your inquiries.'

'That's been more by good fortune than design.'

'Nevertheless it is a fact.'

There was a silence. Then Manton said, 'O.K., Mr. Cape, I don't lock you in, *but* if you do get in my way, nothing will save you from being thrown to the lions. The lions in your case being the governing body of your profession. Is that absolutely clear?'

Adam let out a sigh of relief.

'Fair enough. The risk is all mine.'

'What do you mean by risk? If there's any question of risks, you're staying locked in here.'

'You misunderstood me.'

'I'm glad, because frankly I'm acting against my better judgement. If you bungle things for me tonight . . .'

'I haven't bungled anything yet, and everything I've done has, in fact, helped you.'

'I know, I know, but from now on, Mr. Cape, I don't even want your help.'

Adam sat alone in the hut. It was nearly midnight and though he wasn't sleepy he felt stiff and tired. He would have liked to have stretched his legs round the timber yard but had given Manton an undertaking that he would not leave the hut until told he might.

'The slightest movement and they could be scared off', Manton had said on his own last visit to the hut. 'Once they've gone inside the building opposite, it doesn't matter so much.'

Adam's mind went back over the past fifteen hours. It was difficult to believe that this was still the same day that had started off with a lazy morning spent in respectable Kensington, followed by a swim and a sandwich lunch with Sara.

No wonder he was hungry. He hadn't eaten for nearly twelve hours. And thinking of Sara, she would be home by now. He hoped she wouldn't try and phone him, and find out that he hadn't yet got back.

Manton had asked him if anyone knew where he was and he had replied that only Sara did. And Manton had said, 'Let's hope she doesn't come looking for you, Mr. Cape.'

A faint sound came to his ear. A new sound. That of a car engine revving. Then all was silence once more.

A few minutes later, the hut door opened and Manton entered.

'They've arrived', he said in a quietly triumphant tone.

'How many?'

'Three or four, I should guess, but I couldn't tell properly. They arrived in a closed van. Hapgood got out and let himself through the side door. Then he opened the gates from inside to let the van in.'

'How long will you give them?'

'About half an hour. Just time for them to get their equipment unpacked.'

Adam experienced a sudden quiver of excitement. The stage was being set and soon the curtain would rise to disclose the players.

'Apart from Hapgood, you couldn't see who the others were?'

'No, but it won't be long now before we know.' Manton spoke with the quiet satisfaction of someone who was about to enjoy the fructification of his plans.

'What do you want me to do when you go in after them?'

Manton raised an eyebrow. 'You've given me your word not to interfere, which means in effect you stay this side of the road. Since you ask the question, however, I suggest you remain right here in the hut.'

'That's like taking someone to see the boat-race and then putting them behind a tree.'

'I didn't bring you here, Mr. Cape. You arrived uninvited and, if I may say so, unwanted. You're a trespasser in fact. But don't let's go into all that again. I'm not locking you in and you're not getting in my way. That's our bargain.' He paused. 'Though heaven knows why I should strike bargains with you after what's happened.' He looked at his watch. 'I must leave you. Stick around, Mr. Cape, but keep in the wings. I may need your help later.'

The hut door closed behind Manton with a soft click and Adam was once more left in the darkness with his thoughts.

For twenty minutes he endured his confinement, sitting down, standing up and pacing about in a space smaller than a night-club dance floor. From time to time he peered out of the window, but all he could see was the silhouette of the nearest stack of timber.

He tiptoed across to the door and opened it. A second

later he had stepped outside and was swallowed up by the shadows.

No sound came from any quarter as he moved stealthily in the direction of the road. The yard gave every sign of being deserted and he surmised that Manton and his men must by now be inside the printing works.

He reached the front row of stacks and paused to listen again. Still no sound. Creeping round the edge he could now see a stretch of the road and the back entrance to Mather's premises. The only light came from a flickering street lamp some forty yards farther down. It might have been forty miles for all the illumination it cast where Adam was standing.

He gazed across at the dark outline of the building opposite. Somewhere within its walls a life-and-death game of hide-and-seek was being enacted in the eerie silence of a catacomb.

All of a sudden, he ran across the open forecourt of the timber yard and through the gate by which he had entered. Diving across the road, he sought the shelter of the opposite wall and pressed himself against it, his senses alert for any sound within.

But all he heard was an occasional car speeding in the distance along the main road.

Shuffling crabwise with his back to the wall, Adam made his way towards the door which led into Mathers' back yard. It swung open as he turned the handle and he stepped quickly inside. He had a prickly sensation down his spine as he realized the risk he was running, but the yard was empty apart from the van, which stood facing the closed double gates, obviously parked for a rapid departure.

In the far left-hand corner of the yard stood a door which must lead into the printing works. Adam stared at it undecided on his next move, when suddenly a shot rang out.

It came from somewhere inside the building and was succeeded by a series of sharp whistle blasts, muffled shouts and sounds of running feet.

For a full minute he continued to stare at the door. But as suddenly as there had been the electrifying eruption of sound, all was quiet again.

With even greater caution, Adam now crept towards the inner door, hugging the wall as he went.

He had just reached it, when it burst open and someone came hurtling out with the force of a projectile.

Adam felt himself spinning backwards across the yard. He had managed to get a grip of his assailant's coat and knew that he must hang on to it at all costs, but avoid being crushed beneath him when their reckless progress ended in an inevitable fall.

As his feet slithered away beneath him he twisted his body sideways and let his muscles go loose to break the shock of his impact with the cement floor.

The other man was less fortunate. He thudded full length beside Adam and there was a ghastly crack as his head struck the ground.

Adam rose groggily to his feet as the door thrust open again and three more men came hurtling into the yard.

'There they are, two of 'em', a voice shouted.

A second later, a feebly protesting Adam was seized round the waist in a bear's hug.

'Hold on, Colin, it's that bloke again', said Detective-Sergeant Mackenzie, peering fiercely into Adam's face.

'What are you doing here? I thought Mr. Manton told you to keep right out of it.'

Without waiting for Adam to answer, he knelt down beside the prostrate body on the ground and let out a grunt of satisfaction.

'This is Hapgood, all right.' He looked up at Adam and asked incredulously, 'Did *you* knock him out?'

'He knocked himself out . . . with my assistance.'

Sergeant Mackenzie gave him a puzzled look, then turning to the other two said, 'Colin, you and Jim look after Hapgood. I'll take him' – he nodded his head in Adam's direction – 'to Mr. Manton.'

Adam followed him into the building, where large silent pieces of machinery loomed all about and the air smelt of engine oil.

'Better watch out. Whole place is a ruddy booby trap.'

'Did you catch the others?'

Sergeant Mackenzie grunted. 'Don't know who we've got and who we haven't got.'

'I thought I heard a shot.'

'Too true you did. One of our chaps got a bullet through his shoulder. Mind these stairs. They're covered in grease. Murderous they are.'

Adam felt one foot slide away and clutched at an iron rail for support.

'They greased that too.'

'Who?'

'The chums who came to do the place. Made sure no one could creep up on 'em unheard.'

'How'd your lot get down?' Adam asked, edging his way cautiously forward rather like a novice on skates.

Sergeant Mackenzie let out an oath as he sat down heavily. 'Just like we'd been tipped down a blasted chute, but with more noise. That's what gave the alarm. Lucky we had the numbers. Must have looked like a rugger pack charging 'em.'

'Who fired?'

'Don't know yet.'

They reached the bottom of the stairs and Adam saw that they were in a low-ceilinged basement which housed the heating apparatus.

'Through here', the Sergeant said, leading the way to an open doorway on the other side.

The second room was much larger. It was lit by a naked bulb which hung from the ceiling and cast gloomy shadows round the perimeter of the room.

A small knot of men were standing in one corner like conspirators. As Sergeant Mackenzie and Adam came through the door, Manton, who was one of them, turned his head.

'Who said you could come down here?' he asked disagreeably, as he caught sight of Adam.

Sergeant Mackenzie replied. 'I brought him down, sir. We found him in the yard outside with Hapgood. He'd knocked Gus out.'

Manton's eyes opened wider in patent astonishment.

'That's not quite right', Adam said in an apologetic tone, and proceeded to tell Manton what had happened.

'Well, it seems we have you to thank for his capture whichever way one looks at it', Manton remarked dryly.

'I suppose he'd have attempted a getaway in the van.'

177

'He wouldn't have got very far. We'd removed the rotor arm.'

Adam grinned. Immobilized van and greased stairs! It seemed that the participants on both sides had shown forethought.

'How many have you caught?'

'Two. Care to see them?'

Adam nodded and Manton led the way across the basement and through into a further chamber.

Sitting handcuffed on the floor against the farther wall were Roger Winslow and Frankie Young. Three police officers stood over them.

Winslow's face was an expressionless mask. He was staring straight ahead of him and showed no sign of recognizing Adam or even of being aware of his presence.

Young, on the other hand, presented a very different picture, a mixture of utter dejection and incontinent terror.

Adam found that he was unable to take his eyes off them, for there was something else which scratched furiously to be released from his subconscious. Something which it was vital he should recall, but which was an elusive as a shy maiden's smile.

Baffled, he let his gaze roam on. Not far from where the men sat, stood an oxygen cylinder and safe-blowing equipment.

'How were they going to get into the bank?' he asked in an abstracted tone when the silence had become almost palpable. It was like being in the Chamber of Horrors without the crowds.

'I'll show you.'

Adam followed Manton across the room and saw a hole

178

in the wall at floor level, just big enough to enable a man to crawl through. Broken brick was scattered all about.

'Five yards of tunnel and you're in the bank.'

Adam whistled softly. 'Actually in the bank?'

'As good as', Manton retorted. 'With only a wall no thicker than this one to be penetrated. Another half-hour and they'd have been through into the bank.' He looked dispassionately at Young. 'He obviously discovered the possibility when he was working here and offered himself as a guide. They could never have found the way through without him in this subterranean maze.'

'Do you mean that just the three of them planned this?'

'That', Manton observed grimly, 'is what I'm shortly going to find out. If Gus Hapgood got as far as he did, someone else might have got further. Three is on the short side for a major operation like this. I'd have expected at least four, possibly five, to have been in on it, though not necessarily all round the honey-pot at the same time.'

He turned towards the doorway, as an officer came in and said, 'Car's here now, sir.'

'Good. Take them upstairs and get them back to the station. I'll be along in five minutes.'

One of the officers standing guard over Winslow and Young motioned them to get up.

'Better handcuff them to yourself as well', Manton said.

Adam watched as an officer manacled himself to each prisoner and the four men then left looking like a miniature chain gang.

The officer who had come in spoke again. 'I've also had word, sir, that someone's on their way from Finger-prints and Photographic Branch.'

'The van and that safe-blowing equipment will be the most likely places to find prints', Manton observed. 'In fact there's not much we can do about anywhere else.'

'Didn't they wear gloves?' Adam broke in, surprised at this breach of what he had imagined to be an elementary rule of burglary.

'Yes, but there's always a chance that someone's handled that equipment at some time without gloves. Same thing goes for the van.'

He turned to leave and Adam followed him, pausing in the doorway to recall . . . recall . . . What was it that flitted elusively at the back of his mind, and which had struck some intangible chord of familiarity?

As he accompanied Manton back through the warren-like basement, he vainly explored his mind for some clue which would explain the feeling.

When they emerged into the open, Adam observed that a police car had been backed into the yard and was parked beside the van. Manton walked over to speak to the driver, and a moment later called over his shoulder, 'O.K., Mr. Cape, we'll get along to the station.'

Adam got into the back of the car beside Manton. 'What's going to happen when we get there?'

'As far as I'm concerned, there's a night's work ahead, and the first thing is to interview Young about his wife's death. I'll arrange for a car to take you home as soon as you like. I thought, though, you might like to wait around for a short while and see what happens.' He gave Adam a small, attractive smile. 'A reward for your assistance. Perhaps I should say tenacity.'

The car halted outside the building which housed

Divisional Headquarters and Manton jumped out and
hurried inside.

'Have you got a Mr. Cape with you, sir?' Adam heard
the duty sergeant ask as they passed the inquiry desk.

'This is Mr. Cape. Why?'

'There's a gentleman here who was worried about him.
He's waiting upstairs in the C.I.D. general office.' Adam
shook his head and returned Manton's inquiring look with
an expression of blank surprise. The duty sergeant con-
sulted a piece of paper. 'Mr. Lelaker, that's who he said he
was.'

'Good God, what on earth's Tony doing here?' Adam
exclaimed.

As they reached the C.I.D. office, Tony Lelaker sprang
from the chair in which he'd been sitting.

'Are you all right, Adam? Sara was terribly worried
about your not being home, and told me what you'd pro-
posed doing. I thought it mightn't be a bad idea to call in at
the police station on the way and then I heard something
about a gang and I was about to drive on to Mathers' when
an officer arrived back and said you'd be here soon.' He
gave Adam an admiring look. 'You really have been having
a ball, you lucky old sod. And to think what I've missed!'

Adam smiled sheepishly, and without enthusiasm. On
the whole it was unflattering to have one's friends chasing
after one like anxious nursemaids.

'Superintendent, this is a friend of mine, Mr. Lelaker.'

Manton nodded a greeting and said, 'I'll leave you
together while I go and see to the prisoners. You can go any
time you wish, Mr. Cape.'

'Tell me all that's been happening, Adam', Lelaker said

eagerly when they were alone. He listened intently while Adam gave him a somewhat incoherent précis of events, and at the end asked, 'Did they catch the lot?'

'That's what Manton's hoping to find out now.'

'There was a silence. Then yawning hard, Tony Lelaker said, 'Well, I've had nothing like your adventures, but I'm set for bed. You ready to be driven home?'

'We might as well go. I'll just let Manton know.'

In the corridor he met an officer he recognized and asked him to pass a message to Manton, who, he gathered, had given instructions that he was not to be disturbed. It served somehow to emphasize the policeman's lot when such instructions required to be given at two o'clock in the morning and were not just a card hung outside a bedroom door.

As they drove back into Central London, the air of a warm summer's night rushing past them in the open car, Adam was silent, as he desperately tried to dredge his subconscious for the small vital shining clue to everything which he felt certain lay submerged there.

Luckily, Tony Lelaker seemed content to accept the silence and drove through the deserted streets rapt in thoughts of his own.

Adam woke with a start to find Florence shaking his bare shoulder. He seldom wore a pyjama top and never in the summer.

'There's a policeman downstairs wants to see you', she announced as he blearily opened his eyes. Her rough dry hand remained resting on his shoulder.

'A policeman? What's he want?'

'Just said to wake you up and say it was important.'

'What time is it?'

'Quarter past eight.'

Adam yawned and rolled on to his back. Florence fixed her gaze on his brown chest and sighed.

'Miss Brown won't half carry on, if she finds out. Gives the place a bad name. And on a Sunday morning too.'

'You'd better tell him I'll be down in a minute. How is he, in plain clothes?'

'No, in uniform. He's wearing one of those flat caps. Parked his car right outside the front door, he has, too.'

She continued to hover like a nurse waiting to remove the thermometer from the patient's mouth while Adam yawned again and stretched his muscles beneath the covers.

'Phone never stopped ringing last night', she volunteered. 'First that Mr. Lulusomething . . .'

'Lelaker.'

'That's the one, and then your young lady. Miss Brown had to come down in her dressing-gown. Fancy people ringing at that hour. And you not back anyway.'

Adam made a move to get out of bed. 'I'll explain to Miss Brown later', he said tersely. 'Now, go and tell the police officer that I'll be down in a moment.'

With obvious reluctance, Florence slopped out of the room and Adam jumped up and put on his dressing-gown just as she put her head round the door again.

'I've put him in the dining-room', she said with a pout at Adam's hastily turned back.

A quick look out of the window confirmed that a very official police car was indeed parked immediately outside the front door.

With a sense of growing uneasiness, Adam cleaned his

183

teeth – something he did with unusual frequency – tugged a comb through his hair and went downstairs.

A young, freshly-scrubbed looking police officer was sitting on the edge of one of Miss Brown's chairs. He rose as Adam entered.

'Mr. Cape?'

'Yes.'

'Detective-Superintendent Manton sent me to fetch you, sir.'

'To fetch me?'

'Yes, sir, he'd be glad if you'd come along as soon as possible.'

'I thought at first you'd come to arrest me', Adam said with a feeble grin.

'No, sir', he replied without a flicker.

'Do you know what he wants to see me about?'

'No, sir.'

The officer looked meaningly towards the door and Adam, hoisting his pyjama trousers, said, 'Give me five minutes and I'll go and get dressed.'

'Very well, sir. I'll wait in the car with my colleague.'

Through the window, Adam could see an officer sitting at the wheel.

Five minutes later he had dressed, had a shave of sorts and was descending the stairs two at a time.

As he reached the hall, the phone began ringing and he lifted the receiver without contemplating that the call might not be for him.

'May I speak to Mr. Cape, please?' a voice asked.

'Hello, Sara.'

184

'Oh, Adam, you're back', she exclaimed with relief. 'Are you all right?'

'Yes, I'm fine. Look, Sara . . .'

'Tony and I were both so worried when you weren't home last night. By the way, did Tony find you?'

'Yes.'

'What time did you get back?'

'Around two o'clock.'

'Where on earth had you been all the evening?'

'Look, Sara, I've got to go now. There's a police car waiting. It's all right, I've not done anything', he added hastily as he heard her gasp. 'Superintendent Manton wants to see me urgently. I don't know what about, but I promise I'll phone you as soon as I'm through.'

'We were meant to be driving home this morning', Sara said in a deflated tone.

'Don't worry, we shall probably still be able to. 'Bye darling.'

He put down the receiver and darted out of the house and into the waiting car, which leapt away from the kerb like a greyhound released from its trap.

Divisional headquarters looked solid and enduring in the warm sunshine of an early Sunday morning. Inside, however, there was the acrid odour that told of men who had been working all night.

Adam found Manton in his own office. He was unshaven and his eyes were red-rimmed, and he looked sour and dispirited.

He glanced up as Adam entered.

''Morning, Mr. Cape. You, I can see, have had some sleep since we last met. Lucky fellow!'

Adam made no reply but waited for Manton to go on. After all, he had been rushed across London at breakfast-time on a Sunday morning, to be delivered into Manton's presence, and the least he could expect was some sort of an explanation.

Manton leaned forward and clasped his hands on the desk.

'Whether or not you can help me, I don't know, but the position is that Young is absolutely and unshakeably adamant that he did not murder his wife.'

So what! Adam thought, but said nothing. That was more proof of Young's unsuspected fibre than of his innocence.

'He says that he left the Old Bailey after his acquittal in the company of Gus Hapgood and that he has been held a virtual prisoner until the raid last night.'

'Does he know where he was held?' Adam asked with interest.

'Winslow's garage. Yes, you were right about that, Mr. Cape.' Manton reclasped his hands. 'He says that he was told of his wife's death and reminded, in no uncertain fashion, that he was the chief suspect. His captors promised him that once the bank raid was over, he'd be given his cut and a ticket out of the country. In the event of his not fulfilling his part of the bargain, they told him they would shop him and that he could look forward to a life sentence for murder.'

'Does he know who did murder his wife?'

'No-o, he says not, but I'm coming to that in a moment. He has told us practically everything else, however.'

'Such as?'

'That his wife really did stab herself and then accuse him

of it, in order to prevent his taking part in the raid on the bank, which was planned weeks ago for this particular week-end.'

'You mean he told her what was going to take place?'

'Yes. And when she couldn't dissuade him from taking part she inflicted this injury on herself with the knife and accused him so that he would be nicely tided over the period in jail.'

'Does he know who else was in it apart from Winslow and Hapgood?'

'I'm coming to that, too, in a moment', Manton replied. 'Hapgood was not only his contact man before his arrest and his keeper after he'd been acquitted at the Old Bailey, but he was also the man whom Young originally interested in the idea of doing the bank. Incidentally, Gus is an old hand at this sort of thing.'

'Then it was probably Hapgood who murdered Mrs. Young.'

'Except that oddly enough Young gives him an alibi.'

'Winslow then?' Adam frowned in concentrated thought and exclaimed, 'Yes, that's right, it must have been Winslow. Don't you remember my telling you how he brushed into me when Carole Young tried to speak to me after the case was over? He obviously must have realized she was ready to spill the beans and so he followed her home and killed her.' He observed Manton's faintly sceptical expression. 'I don't mean that he actually followed her home. But he sent her that note in my name and lured her to the place where he strangled her.' With new eagerness, he gazed across at Manton's now expressionless face. 'That fits, doesn't it?'

'Yes.' The tone was equally expressionless.

187

'Does Young think it was Winslow who murdered his wife?'

'Until they found themselves handcuffed together, Young had never seen Winslow.'

'What on earth do you mean?'

'Simply that when Young was fetched out of his cell last night – the cell in which the gang had been keeping him – a bag was put over his head and he was bundled into the back of the van. When they got inside the bank, he was given a mask to enable him to see, and what he did see was that his three fellow conspirators were similarly hooded. He was able to recognize Hapgood by his general figure, but as I say, he'd never set eyes on Winslow's face until our intervention.' He paused and added dryly, 'I don't think I told you that we found them with hoods over their heads.'

Adam slowly shook his head. He was puzzled.

'Did you say there were *three* others with him?'

'I did.'

'Hapgood and Winslow, but who was the third?'

'Young doesn't know; I don't know. Do you, Mr. Cape?'

CHAPTER NINETEEN

Adam felt as though he had been whipped a blow in the solar plexus. His mind seemed to have become a great echoing chamber in which Manton's clear tones were the only sound. *Do you? Do you?*

The bright blue eyes were fixed firmly on his face and he knew that every second he failed to respond was being recorded in a brain trained to register every seismographic nuance.

When he did speak, he was surprised and gratified to discover that his voice sounded quite normal.

'Of course, I don't. I haven't an idea. Why on earth should you suppose that *I* might know?'

'As a result of something which he overheard, Young seems to think that it was somebody connected with his trial.'

'But that's absolutely absurd. He's obviously been watching too much television if he thinks that prosecuting counsel go about murdering the wives of people who get off.'

'Sounds silly put that way, doesn't it?' Manton agreed.

'Sounds utterly fantastic put any way.'

'But of course there were others connected with the trial apart from yourself.' Manton smiled deprecatingly. 'It was you who immediately jumped to the conclusion that I was referring to yourself. I didn't say so.'

'You insinuated it.'

Manton brushed the accusation aside.

'I take it you know Mr. Imrey fairly well. You're in the same chambers, aren't you?'

'You're not seriously suggesting that Charles Imrey had anything to do with it?'

'I'm not suggesting anything', Manton said tersely. 'I'm merely probing. How well do you know Mr. Imrey?'

'I've known him for about two years. He's a person of the highest integrity.'

'I see. You've been to his home?'

'Not actually.'

'But you know his friends and what he does when he's not working?' Adam gave him a stony stare. 'Well, do you?'

'No, I don't know him socially other than over the occasional pint of beer.'

'So you don't know him very well, do you?' Manton passed a hand across his face. 'I'm sorry, Mr. Cape, but I'm tired and I get a bit irritated by all this irresponsible rushing to the defence of someone you don't *really* know.'

'O.K., but I'm still quite certain', Adam began and then stopped abruptly as he suddenly called to mind Charles Imrey's last-minute change of plan whereby he had stayed in town over the week-end instead of driving down to Devon on the Friday. Indeed, that had been the very day on which he had received the mysterious telephone call which he had been so anxious that Adam should not overhear. Charles Imrey, so suave, so self-possessed, so well-groomed . . . surely it wasn't possible . . .

'Yes, Mr. Cape, what are you quite certain about?'

Adam blushed. 'You can't really believe that Charles Imrey had anything to do with it', he said in a weak voice.

Manton studied him in thoughtful silence for several seconds, then observed dispassionately, 'In my job one can believe anything of anyone, given the faintest reason for doing so.'

Adam shook his head slowly, bewildered by his own thoughts.

'If you're determined to suspect someone who was connected with the case, what about the solicitor, Creedy?'

'I can't quite picture him taking part in a bank robbery. He's over sixty, you know, which virtually rules him out. You need to be fit and tough, and Creedy's neither.'

'Well, I can only suggest that Young has got hold of the wrong end of the stick. That is, if you believe him at all, which I gather you do.'

Adam's mind drifted back to the scene in Mather Brothers' basement the previous night. What was it that had touched that chord of hazy recollection at the back of his mind? He tried to visualize it as it was when he had first entered with Manton and had seen Young and Winslow sitting there in dejection, handcuffed together. But for the present, the chance of identifying the missing piece of the puzzle seemed more remote than ever.

'Have Hapgood or Winslow talked?' he asked, when he could think no further. Manton shook his head.

'Neither's said a word. The devil of it is that I can't play off Young against them either, since they knew in advance exactly how much he'd be able to say, and probably would say.'

'So what you want is some clue as to who it was that lured Carole Young out of her house and murdered her? Young, Hapgood, Winslow or—?'

'X'. Manton drummed his fists on the desk. 'I've got to know who was X, Mr. Cape, and you're going to help me.'

'How?'

'By going over once again every detail of what you did on the evening of the murder.'

'How's that going to help?'

'Listen, Mr. Cape', Manton said with weary patience. 'A few years ago I was in charge of inquiries in a murder case in the provinces. Two weeks went by and I was nowhere. I'd done everything I could think of, interviewed every person who might provide information, spent so much time staring at the scene of the crime that I could describe each blade of grass to you now, and still I'd got nowhere. The Press had written it off as unsolved, the local Chief Constable, who had called in the Yard, clearly wondered why he had bothered, and all in all there couldn't have been a stronger atmosphere of frustration and futility. I was completely at my wits' end – I had returned to London for a couple of days – when I happened to run into George Palmer. I don't suppose you've ever heard of him, but he used to be Chief Detective-Superintendent at Number 3 District before he retired. He knew just about as much as all the rest put together, of a detective's job. I told him my troubles – he'd read all about the case in the papers – and asked him his advice, hoping, I suppose, for some brilliant piece of insight which would put me on the right track to solving the case.

'He listened quietly and when I had finished and said, "Well, George, any suggestions?" he replied, "Yes, certainly. There's only one thing you can do. Start from the beginning again and go over everything. *Everything.*"

'I may add that I didn't thank him for his advice until

some weeks later, when we happened to meet and an arrest had been made, largely through doing what George Palmer had suggested.

'I think that should answer your question, Mr. Cape.'

Adam assumed an expression of quiet surrender, and in a dull monotone began to recite the events of that fateful evening – the evening, as it now occurred to him, of his first major indiscretion. Even as the thought passed across the back of his mind, his tone quickened. Indiscretion? He had nothing to regret or apologize for.

'. . . and I just had time to see the note on the table and register the fact that it was signed in my name before I heard footsteps in the passage outside and had to dive for cover.'

'What else was there on the table?' Manton asked with sudden interest.

'I can't remember', Adam replied after a moment's pause.

'Try to. For example, was there a handbag there?'

'I don't recall seeing one. I have an idea there was a cup and saucer at the other side of the table.'

'But the note was quite alone?'

'Yes, I'm sure it was. It was lying open by itself. That's why it immediately caught my attention. I mean it wasn't partially hidden under anything, if that's what you're thinking.'

Manton nodded. 'Mmm. I see. Go on. You dived for cover behind the curtain partition. What then?'

'Well, I heard someone come into the room. I heard them breathe a sort of sigh and a second later the door was shut and they'd gone.'

'You didn't see them at all? Not even a toe-cap or a finger-nail?'

'No, definitely not.'

'And when you emerged from your hiding-place?'

'The note had gone.'

'As far as you could tell, had anything else been touched?'

'No, but my chief concern then was to get out of the house. Anyway the whole incident was no more than her coming into the room to pick up the note and then leaving again.'

'You say "her". You mean Carole Young?'

'Yes, there was the faint smell of perfume after she'd gone out.'

'But not before. You didn't notice anything when you first entered the room?'

Adam jerked upright as though a thousand volts of electricity had suddenly passed down his spinal column.

'That's it!' he cried exultantly. 'That's what I've been trying to recall. The smell.' He gave Manton an excited look. 'That's what I noticed in Mather's basement last night, in that room where you had Winslow and Young.'

'What did you notice?' Manton asked with a frown.

'The same smell as there'd been in Carole Young's room after the note had gone.'

There was a pause while each digested this piece of information.

'Well, at least one thing is certain', Manton said at length. 'And that is that Carole Young wasn't taking part in any bank robbery last night.'

'Then it couldn't have been she who came back for the note.'

'Precisely. More likely to have been the murderer after

he had strangled her and discovered that the note was not in her handbag. He decided to see if she had left it at the house.' Adam shivered, and Manton went on, 'Presumably, so far as the murderer is aware, only he and his victim would ever have seen the note. Hence his desire, if possible, to regain possession of it and destroy it.'

'You keep on saying "he", Superintendent. But men don't use perfume.'

'After-shave lotions? Hair-creams? And anyway this was not a woman's crime. You're quite certain that you noticed the same smell again last night?'

'Absolutely. I knew there was something familiar as soon as I went into that room where they were. And I've been trying ever since to think what it was. It was a fainter smell, but definitely the same.'

Manton got up. 'We can soon put this to a test.' His voice held a note of suppressed excitement. 'Winslow, Young and Hapgood are downstairs in the cells, and you can go and take a good sniff at each.'

As they went downstairs and Manton collected the key, Adam's stomach felt as full of butterflies as it had on the morning of Young's trial. The last twenty-four hours had been like an endless unreal dream, induced by a whiff of some new nerve gas.

Manton unlocked the iron grills which led to the row of cells, six on each side of a whitewashed passage.

He stopped at the first, slid back the panel which covered a peep-hole, and said, 'Just look at him.'

Lying on his back with his mouth open and his eyes closed, was Gus Hapgood.

'He's not dead, is he?' Adam asked anxiously.

'Dead! You can hear his snores through six inches of mortar.'

Manton unlocked the cell door and with a climactic grunt, Hapgood opened his eyes and with surprising agility leapt up off his hard bed.

'It's O.K., Gus, you can go back to sleep again', Manton said and nodded to Adam to enter. 'I think you know Mr. Cape – at any rate by sight.'

Hapgood's eyes became expressionless as warily he watched the two men at his cell door.

Adam stepped in and surreptitiously sniffed the air, which was fetid and not unlike that of a barrack-room with a dozen soldiers peeling off their clothes after a long route march.

One look at the top of Hapgood's grizzled head refuted the idea of any use of hair-cream.

Adam left the cell with relief. As Manton relocked the door, he remarked, 'You'd need a gallon of Eau-de-Cologne to overcome the odours in there. We'll try Young next.'

As before, he invited Adam to take a peep at the unsuspecting prisoner before they revealed themselves.

Young was sitting on his bed, head in hands, staring at the opposite wall with an expression of utter despair in every line of his face.

He turned his head as he heard the key in the lock but didn't otherwise move.

A puzzled, and further worried look, came into his eyes as he recognized Adam. For his own part, Adam felt grimly uncomfortable in the presence of such naked panic. Even as he returned Young's gaze, he observed beads of perspiration forming on his upper lip and above his chin.

Young's hair was unkempt and greasily dirty. To Adam's distaste, Manton rubbed a hand over it and held it up to Adam's nose after sniffing at it himself.

Outside the cell, he said, 'Nothing very fresh or perfumed about that.'

'No', Adam agreed, hating the whole business more than ever.

'There's only Winslow left. He's in the end one on the right.'

Roger Winslow was lying on his bed staring at the ceiling with hands clasped beneath his head, and only his eyes moved as they entered his cell. He showed no sign of recognizing Adam, but cast Manton a coldly arrogant look.

'You don't seem as much in need of a bath as your companions', Manton remarked, taking a deep breath.

'Is this some new ploy?' Winslow asked with a faint sneer. 'Have you sent a message to my solicitor that I wish to see him?'

'Difficult to get hold of him, you know', Manton replied vaguely. 'Sunday of the Bank Holiday week-end. Offices shut. People away from home.'

Winslow's lip curled. 'I'm not bothered about the holiday habits of the great British public. I just wish to see my solicitor, Mr. Creedy. I know his office is shut on Sundays, but he has a home and a telephone, though I take it from your evasive answer that you've made no attempt to get hold of him for me.'

'We will do', Manton said.

'Well, you needn't think that I'll suddenly break down and make a statement just by holding me incommunicado.'

Manton gazed at him levelly. 'You'll have your solicitor

all in good time. There's nothing yet which says that a police officer's first duty is to send for the prisoner's legal adviser. Before you appear in court tomorrow, you'll have seen Mr. Creedy, so don't try and order me around.'

While this dialogue had been taking place, Adam had been quietly sniffing the air in the cell, though without any interest to his olfactory senses. Though Winslow had a light stubble on his chin and upper lip, his hair, which was in need of a cut, was neatly combed and apparently without any dressing.

When they were in the corridor outside again, Manton gave Adam an inquiring look. 'Another blank?'

''Fraid so.'

'You could have imagined the smell last night.'

'I'm sure I didn't.'

They left the cells and went back to Manton's room, where he sent for Detective-Sergeant Mackenzie.

When the officer arrived, Manton said, 'Mac, I want you to round up everyone who was with us last night. Bring them along to my room.'

'Some of 'em have gone off duty now, sir. Do you want them fetched too?'

'No, only those who happen to be in the building.'

Ten minutes later, Sergeant Mackenzie returned with three other officers. 'I'm afraid this is all, sir.'

'May be enough.' Manton looked at the four faces lined against the wall of his office. Though their eyes were watchful, their expressions gave nothing away. Manton smiled at them almost shyly and said, 'Did any of you smell anything down in Mathers' basement last night? Glover?'

The officer on his far left shook his head. 'No, sir.'

'Polley?'

'Gas, do you mean, sir?'

'Anything?'

'No, sir.'

'Lane?'

'Well, now you mention it, sir, I think I did notice an odd trace of scent, but I'm afraid I didn't give it much of a thought at the time.'

'What sort of scent?'

Detective Constable Lane's brow puckered as he pondered the question.

'Can't describe it any more, sir. Just scent.'

'Did it occur to you at the time where it might come from?'

To Adam's surprise, the officer, who didn't look more than twenty, blushed furiously and cast an anxious glance down the line of his colleagues.

'Well, actually, sir, I thought it was D.C. Polley's new after-shave lotion what he's been using since he became engaged.'

Laughter rippled down the line at this suggestion, only D.C. Polley himself refraining. He set his features in a sheepish grin, however, after a furious glare at his friend.

'Had you used some of your new after-shave lotion last night, Polley?' Manton inquired.

'I had not, sir. I don't use it when I'm going on duty.'

When they had left the room Manton turned to Adam and said, 'You have support after all. Detective-Constable Lane bears out what you say – or smelt.'

'But who . . . who was giving off the blessed smell?'

'Clearly "X". X. who murdered Carole Young. X. who

199

was present on the raid last night but who managed to escape.'

'Without anyone knowing who he is.'

'On the contrary, two people know quite well who he is. Winslow and Hapgood.'

'But they won't talk.'

'No, and if I can't persuade them to tell me directly, I must get it out of them indirectly.'

But, in fact, it never became necessary for Manton to direct his wits to this end.

CHAPTER TWENTY

IN THE silence that followed Manton's last observation, the truth slowly seeped through Adam's brain, though it was still some time before he was able to recognize it for what it was.

His mind at first failed to recognize it and then blankly refused to. It was as though he had suddenly been given a piece of shattering news. In the numbness which followed the immediate shock, his mind sought to find refuge if not in actual disbelief, at least in the peripheral irrelevancies of the new situation.

Although it had not been until this morning that he had realized it was a smell which connected two events for him, he now felt that it would be in his nostrils for ever.

He had carried it with him after leaving Mather Brothers' basement. He had, he now knew, smelt it again when he had arrived at the police station the previous night – or rather in the early hours of the present morning.

He had not consciously registered it then because he had still not identified the chord of familiarity it subsequently evoked.

Now, slowly and painfully he forced himself to face the whole bowel-opening truth. He was aware that Manton was staring at him with a curious expression.

'You feeling all right, Mr. Cape?'

He swallowed and nodded, and in a voice which he scarcely recognized as his own, said, 'Were Winslow and the others brought up here yesterday evening?'

'I spent the night interviewing them in this room.'

'But were they in the C.I.D. general office?'

'Yes. While I saw each of them in turn in this room, other officers were interviewing them in the general office. Why?'

'Was that after I had left?' Adam's voice seemed to indicate an anxiety that his words might disintegrate before reaching Manton's ears.

'Long after.'

Adam closed his eyes and felt suddenly physically hollow. It was like the moment before one underwent major surgery from which survival was judged to be uncertain.

It was, without warning or preparation, the moment of truth.

'I don't quite know how I'm going to tell you this, Superintendent.'

Manton looked up from the piece of paper on which he was scribbling some notes. 'Tell me what?'

'I think I know who X. is.'

CHAPTER TWENTY-ONE

IT TOOK Adam twenty minutes to unburden himself.
Twenty minutes during which Manton's eyes never left
his face and which in every way were the worst of his life.
Even the first occasion he had stood up in a court and
pleaded, paled into insignificance compared with his present
agony.

This time it was his own sense of security which had been
savagely ripped away, leaving him as unprotected as a snail
deprived of its shell.

When he finished, Manton was pensively silent for over a
minute. Then picking up his pencil, he asked, 'How do you
spell his name?'

Adam passed his tongue across his lips. 'Lelaker.
L-E-L-A-K-E-R.'

CHAPTER TWENTY-TWO

N O ANSWER', Manton remarked as he put the telephone receiver back on its cradle. 'Would you
expect him to be at home at half past ten on a
Sunday morning?'

Adam nodded slowly and as though in a dream.

'Is he married?'

'He has a girl-friend.'

'A resident girl-friend, you mean?'

'Yes.' Adam's mind flew to Debbie as he wondered just
how much she knew of what had been going on. Manton's
voice broke into his thoughts.

'I'll send Detective-Sergeant Mackenzie to make some
inquiries at the flats where he lives.'

So it was, that in less than half an hour a message came
back that Mr. Lelaker and his friend had left the flat at first
light that morning and had not been seen since.

Manton received the news with a grunt.

'He must have thought that Winslow or Hapgood might
shop him.'

'But they've shown no intention of doing so.'

'Yet.' He lifted the telephone receiver. 'Have Winslow
brought up to my office, Sergeant.'

While they were waiting, Manton got up and went and
stared out of the window. At the sound of footsteps outside

in the corridor, he turned to Adam and said, 'You go and sit over in that corner away from my desk.'

Winslow entered, manacled to D.C. Lane.

'I believe you're a friend of Tony Lelaker's. Is that right?' Manton asked casually.

Winslow stiffened and glanced quickly but unmistakably in Adam's direction.

'Yes, Mr. Cape knows him as well. He seems to have disappeared. Was that all part of the plan, to leave you holding the baby?'

'I don't know what you're talking about. I don't know anyone named Lelaker. I wish to see my solicitor.' Winslow spoke in jerks like a phrase book.

'O.K., take him back to his cell', Manton said wearily. He looked at his watch. 'Well, it may be Sunday for you, Mr. Cape, but it's a working day as far as I'm concerned. I'd be grateful if you'd keep in touch with me. Are you going out of London?'

Adam tried to remember what his plans were. 'Yes, I was supposed to be driving down to Suffolk to stay with my girl-friend's parents.'

'How long for?'

'Only till Tuesday.'

'Will you come back sooner if I ask you to?'

'Yes.'

'Very well. Just write down the address and telephone number on that bit of paper, would you?'

'That all you want?'

'That's all, Mr. Cape. Though you might spare me a thought as you drive through the green country-side with a pretty girl at your side. I'll be in touch with you in a day or so, if not before. I not only have to try and find your friend Lelaker, but I also have to dig up some evidence. I wouldn't like the whole case to rest on your sense of smell.'

CHAPTER TWENTY-THREE

A S SARA and Adam drove down to Suffolk later that day in the car which Sara's aunt had lent them, their conversation came in spasmodic bursts.

Sara had been stunned by the news, and for long spells of the run they drove in silence, each obsessed by his own thoughts which would suddenly break through the surface of the mind and be expressed aloud.

'But he was such an easy, charming person', Sara said, casting an unhappy look at a field of placidly-munching cows.

Adam sighed. 'I suppose he's always been an outlaw by nature, but outlaws are not necessarily all black. In fact they frequently have great charm. Look at' – here he mentioned the names of two notorious playboys whose charm had recently proved to be their downfall – 'both charmers, but both in prison for all that.'

'But they didn't kill anyone', Sara said. 'It's the fact that Tony could murder that poor girl in cold blood that I find so horrible. That wasn't the act of a gay buccaneer, but of a pitiless executioner.'

'I know. He must have been born minus something.'

'Minus a heart, if you ask me. And the way, too, he embroiled you in his plans! To think how he engineered that first meeting you had in the coffee-bar.'

Adam nodded grimly. 'Manton's certain about it. He'd found out I was prosecuting Young, observed that I often called in there when I left chambers in the evening and then just planted himself so that it appeared that I came upon him and not the other way about.'

'And I suppose it was he who also sent you those anonymous notes?'

'Yes. He must have hoped that he could stall the prosecution before the case reached trial. It was a pretty stupid thing to try and do.'

'But was it, Adam? After all, even if the case did go ahead, he still might have succeeded in shaking your view of it.'

'My God, you're right.' Adam's jaw dropped. 'You don't think he can believe that Young was acquitted because I pulled my punches as a result of those notes?'

'Anyway you didn't, so what's it matter', Sara replied warmly.

There was a brief silence as Adam overtook a lorry through a cloud of diesel fumes. Then he said :

'The irony of it is that the notes *were* true. Carole Young *was* making a false accusation.'

'Fancy being reduced to turning a knife on yourself and accusing your husband in order to save him from something worse. . . .' Sara blinked away a tear. 'What would Young have got if he had been convicted?'

'I should say twelve months at the most. He might even have got away with a conditional discharge, and not gone to prison at all. Anyway, far less than he'll get for taking part in the raid on the bank. That'll probably earn him nearer five years.'

'And do you really think the others will try and pin his wife's murder on to him?'

'I imagine Winslow and Hapgood will wait and see which way things go. It also depends on what happens if and when the police find Tony. On the face of it, Young's still a suspect, with motive and opportunity.'

'But you said he had an alibi.'

'One that depends on Hapgood, and *he* hasn't yet given any indication whether he intends to support it. And even if he does, one criminal alibi-ing another isn't very persuasive. However, that's all fairly academic if, in fact, Tony committed the murder.'

He gave her a rueful grin and she slipped her hand on to his knee and rested it there for the next few miles.

Adam half expected to find a message from Manton waiting for him, demanding his immediate return to London. But there was none; nor did one come the next day, which he and Sara spent lying in the sun on the bank of a small stream which ran through the Slomans' property.

It was ineffably peaceful and under its spell the events of the preceding days slowly fell into perspective.

It was as they were lying on the grass side by side with fingers gently intertwined that Adam became aware that he was returning to normal.

He moved his head and gazed in quiet satisfaction at Sara's upturned face. Her eyes were closed, her lips were slightly parted and her fair hair fell back from her brow.

He rolled gently over on to his side and like a butterfly taking its time to settle on a summer flower moved his head slowly closer towards hers until their lips met.

. . . . .

209

The next afternoon they drove back to London. Adam had scanned the morning papers for news of Lelaker, but there was nothing apart from a short factual paragraph stating that three men had appeared at North London Magistrates' Court, charged with breaking and entering the premises of Mather Brothers and had been remanded in custody for a week. The police had informed the magistrate that further charges were likely and that another man might be involved. That was all.

It seemed obvious that Tony Lelaker had not yet been found, but there was no mention of what steps were being taken to trace him.

Moreover, there was still no message from Manton, when he arrived back at his lodgings that evening.

'Anyone tried to get hold of me while I've been away, Flo?' he asked, after he had taken his bag up to his bedroom.

'Only that friend of yours with the funny name.'

Adam stared at her in disbelief. 'Mr. Lelaker, you mean?'

'Yes, that's the one.'

'What did he want?'

'He wanted you.'

'I know, but did he say where he was or why he wanted me?'

'No', Flo snapped, obviously nettled by the insistence of his questions. 'And it wasn't none of my business to ask him.'

'When was this?'

'About nine o'clock on Sunday evening. I'd just made myself a cup of tea and sat down.'

'Thanks, Flo.' He turned to go back to his room. 'He never phoned again?'

'No, because I told him you wouldn't be home till tonight.'

'But he gave you his name?'

'He didn't have to. I recognized his voice.' She caught Adam's look. 'I'm not as daft as some people take me for.'

'I've always regarded you as brilliant and beautiful', he said, patting her behind and running quickly upstairs.

When he reached chambers the next morning, the first thing he looked for was a letter. It had occurred to him that having failed to reach him on the phone, Tony Lelaker might have decided to write. The more he had thought of it, the more he had come to expect it, but there was none. At least, not one from Tony.

'Had a good week-end, sir?' William asked.

'Yes, thanks, William.'

Adam tried to picture his clerk's face if he should now tell him just how part of it had been spent. It would doubtless match in disapproval the expressions in some of the portraits which hung in Hall.

He paused on the threshold of his room and sniffed. There was nothing perfumed about its atmosphere, however. It was redolent of baked leather and dust, and reminded him that the window must be opened if he was not to suffocate.

Charles Imrey's table was bare, apart from a neatly stacked pile of papers, bound with pink tape. Adam glanced at it and shuddered when he saw that it was a civil bankruptcy case. Good luck to him!

He could picture how outraged Charles would be if he knew that his name had come up as a murder suspect, particularly as Adam now learnt the innocent explanation of his postponed journey to Devon, and of his mysterious telephone call.

The letter which William had handed to him on his arrival a few minutes before was from Charles Imrey. It contained, to Adam's stunned surprise, an apology for possible rudeness the previous Friday and an account of how his wife had been taken suddenly ill with a complaint (unspecified) about which he had been very worried at the time. This had necessitated a postponement of their journey and he, Charles, had come into chambers that morning to receive a call from the specialist who had examined his wife – a call which neither he nor the doctor wished her to know about. As it turned out, he wrote, the whole thing had been a false alarm and all was now well. He hoped Adam had had a good week-end. . . .

Adam permitted himself a wry smile as he tore the letter into small pieces.

Despite the clerk's forebodings at his not returning to chambers till Wednesday morning, he found no work awaiting him, and sat down at his table wondering how he was going to pass a difficult day.

There were, of course, always the current 'law reports', but somehow he felt less in the mood than usual to peruse these. He could imagine Charles Imrey, however, sitting in a deck-chair in his swimming-trunks, an old hat shielding his eyes, as he imbibed the latest authoritative decisions on the interpretation of the Rent Acts.

About half past eleven he could bear it no longer and

picked up the telephone and did what he had been itching to do for the past hour, which was to put through a call to Manton.

He could tell as soon as the connexion was made that the Superintendent was in a sunny mood.

'Yes, what can I do for you, Mr. Cape?' he asked with a faint trace of amusement in his tone.

'I thought I ought to let you know that Lelaker apparently tried to ring me on Sunday evening. He didn't leave any message, but the maid at my digs recognized his voice.'

'I'll ask him what he wanted.'

'You'll . . . you mean you've arrested him?' Adam again felt the pit of his stomach fall away.

'We've located him, Mr. Cape. He was stopping at a cottage in the Cotswolds. The local bobby recognized him from a description we'd sent out. He's on his way back to London at this moment.' There was a pause and Manton added in a sardonic tone, 'You'll probably see in the evening papers that time-honoured euphemism about his assisting the police in their inquiries.'

'Was his girl with him?'

'Debbie? Yes, she's now a brunette, I understand.'

'I suppose it must have been Tony who was carrying the gun that night, since you didn't find one on any of the others?'

'I would deduce that.'

Adam was staring at the wall, hardly aware of Manton's reply as he pursued his own thoughts. 'I still can't understand why he came to the station pretending to look for me. Surely he was running a colossal risk!'

'You provided him with a convenient excuse to be at hand

213

and see what was going to happen, though I think that was of secondary importance. His real reason for coming was to make contact with Winslow.'

'Whatever for?'

'To give him something.'

'What?'

'A useful little gadget, guaranteed to open almost any lock.'

'You mean you found that on Winslow?'

'Yes.'

'But he might have had it all the time.'

'He might have, but he didn't. All three of them were searched in the basement before they were brought to the station and then they were searched again more thoroughly after they'd reached here. This particular little toy was concealed in the hollow sidepiece of a pair of sun-spectacles.'

'Couldn't it have been there all along?'

'The officer who searched him in the basement,' Manton continued patiently, 'is absolutely certain that he didn't have any sun-spectacles on him. Q.E.D. he obtained them later, Q.E.D. from your friend Lelaker. Indeed that's what Winslow says.'

'You've got him to talk then?' Adam exclaimed, now understanding why Manton sounded so pleased with himself.

'Yes, he's talked.'

'How'd you manage it, or is that a very indiscreet question, Superintendent?'

Manton laughed lightly. 'It was really Mr. Creedy who showed him where his best interests lay, that is, after I'd had

214

a word with his solicitor, and pointed out that there was a murder charge hanging about, and that his client was under suspicion.'

'Was he?'

'Of course he was. We could prove that he eavesdropped when Carole Young tried to talk to you in the Old Bailey corridor. And it was clearly he who flashed a warning to Lelaker, telling him that she was likely to spill the beans about the planned bank robbery. Lelaker did the rest.'

'How does Winslow know Tony murdered her?' Adam asked.

'Lelaker told him he'd see to her, and the next thing is she's found in the canal', Manton replied. 'It all supports what your sense of smell told us, Mr. Cape.'

Adam made a slight grimace into the receiver. He could just picture defending counsel cross-examining him on his sense of smell, and without very much difficulty, making him look a complete fool with trayloads of small bottles.

'Tell me, Mr. Cape, would you say that bottle "B" gives off the same aroma as bottle "J", or would you think it more similar to that of bottle "F" . . . Don't be nervous, Mr. Cape, the jury want to know about your sense of smell. We all do, Mr. Cape . . .' and so on. Adam hauled his mind back.

'Have you yet discovered the link between Tony Lelaker and Winslow?' he asked.

'Gather they've known each other a number of years and have worked the odd racket together, though this was to have been their first incursion into major crime. Gus Hapgood's an employee of Winslow's; worked in his garage.

He's a real craftsman with the old oxy-acetylene outfit, incidentally. Done time for safe-blowing. When Young put the suggestion to him that the bank would be an easy proposition when Mather Brothers were closed for the summer holidays, he passed it on to Winslow who brought in Lelaker as the boss, and so the plan came to be made. And that's about it.'

There was a silence before Adam said suspiciously, 'You never told me on Sunday morning that you'd found a skeleton key on Winslow.'

'There were several things I didn't tell you, Mr. Cape', Manton replied smoothly. 'To be absolutely frank, it's only since Winslow's talked that I've become completely satisfied you're wholly on the side of the angels.'

Adam gasped. 'You're pulling my leg.'

'No, I'm not. After all, you must admit that you've behaved in a very suspicious manner on several occasions. And finally there you were lurking around Mathers' place just before the raid took place. It was all highly suspicious – or at least shall I say ambiguous conduct. However, you've certainly helped to solve the case and though you're quite unlike any other barrister I've ever met, let me wish you all the best.' He paused and added dryly, 'I shall certainly follow your career with great interest.'

A second later he had rung off.

Adam was still staring at a far distant horizon five minutes later, when William came into the room. He wore a pleased, I-told-you-so look.

'The Solicitor's Branch at the Yard have just been on the phone, sir. Wanted to know if you'd be able to do an unlawful wounding at London Sessions on Friday. The brief's on its way round now. They must have been pleased, sir, with the way you did that other case.'

He did not appear to notice the small, hollow chuckle his remark caused Adam.

THE END

>>> If you've enjoyed this book and would like to discover more great vintage crime and thriller titles, as well as the most exciting crime and thriller authors writing today, visit: >>>

The Murder Room
Where Criminal Minds Meet

themurderroom.com